Death in the Valley

A Western Frontier Adventure

Book 2 of the Moses Calhoun Mountain Westerns

◊

Robert Peecher

For information the author may be contacted at

PO Box 967; Watkinsville GA; 30677

or at mooncalfpress.com

ISBN: 9781652345398

FOR JEAN

PEECHER

- 1 -

A harsh wind cut through the streets of the town, blowing in from the west with such gusto that the men in the street kept their hats only by mashing them down tight on their heads and holding them in place.

A lone man in a bearskin coat emerged from the trading post, both arms burdened with two large parcels. His hat, an old beaver skin hat with flaps over his ears, remained in place because he'd tied twine over the top of it and under his chin. Were it not for the twine, the hat or the parcels would have to surrender.

The trading post barely deserved such a name, though it dated back several years to a time when it stood as the lone structure in this valley town. Then it was equal parts trading post, saloon, brothel, and post office, though the man who held the position of postmaster back then was seldom called to service. Most of his patrons could neither read nor write, and mail seldom found its way so far out, anyway.

Now the trading post served as a spot for the mountain trappers to bring their pelts for something approaching a reasonable price and get, in exchange, the provisions that would see them through the winter – salt and flour, powder and shot.

Other men built up other stores in the town. The postmaster found himself replaced some years ago by a man with a new store who sold goods freighted in from the south. A new saloon opened with a new brothel; a tavern opened with rooms for travelers. A store in town sold hardware, and another store sold dry goods, and still another store sold groceries. The man at the trading post who at one time possessed not just a corner on the market but all four corners, now did his trade almost exclusively with men from the mountains and mostly in pelts and blankets, though he still sold a fair bit of salt and flour, powder and shot to those who refused to venture into the newer establishments.

Hunched over his packages, dressed in a heavy bearskin coat and his beaver hat, the man looked less like a man and more like an animal lumbering against the wind.

He noted the chill in the wind and wondered if he'd see snow come morning. If not by in the morning, the snow seemed intent on turning up early this year.

He made his way along the road. The rains the previous week had still not dried up, and road through the center of town was a mire of mud and puddles. The wet made everything feel much colder.

At the edge of town, he cut down a worn trail leading out across a wide meadow through the center of the valley. His destination was nestled in among a grove of aspen trees, and they still held some of their glorious yellow leaves – just a last bit of color on the earth before everything turned white and gray and miserable.

The whole way out through the meadow, the man remained oblivious of the four men who had followed him out of the trading post.

If the four men made any noise, the wind whipped it away and drowned it out.

Concerned over his parcels, and intent on keeping his head down into the wind, the man never looked over his shoulder. Not that he had any cause to. The man knew the town to be a safe place in a country overrun with dangers. But most of those dangers walked on four legs and not two, and they could be deeper in the mountains.

Seeing him coming, two young Indian boys who should have been wearing coats rushed out of the cabin and took the parcels from the hunched man. The boys were too young to give a thought to the four men coming out across the meadow.

Moments later, the four men forced their way into the cabin.

Two of them used their Bowie knives on the man in the bearskin coat.

They ignored the parcels and the two Indian boys, but they killed the man.

There was an Indian woman inside the cabin, too. They might have used their knives against the woman as well, except that even in the dim light of the cabin they could see she was a pretty woman. Her bronze skin had no blemishes. Her black hair was held at the back in a long braid. But her eyes, though wide with fright, flashed a pale blue that matched the eyes of the man they killed.

So they took the woman.

One of the men reached inside the dead man's bearskin coat until he found a small leather pouch that rattled with coins. He looked inside it.

"How much?" one of the men asked him.

"About thirty dollars," he answered.

The first man made a derisive grunt.

"Probably the old bastard's life savings. Let's get out of here."

Then, turning to the other two men, he said, "Bring that woman. We can probably sell her to some trapper, or maybe an Injun chief. And if we can't sell her, I bet we can make some good use out of her."

- 2 -

Moses Calhoun watched the five riders cutting out through the valley from a rocky ledge above them.

They had with them a couple of pack mules, and they were not making fast tracks across the valley.

The autumnal wind cutting up from the valley and sweeping across the ledge brought a surprising bite of winter chill. Calhoun didn't expect to feel that cold for another couple of weeks, yet here it was, blowing through him.

If clouds showed in the sky, they'd be in for an early

snow.

Calhoun recognized the man out front of the party in the valley by the way he rode his horse. In a place so void of people, an observant man quickly learned the habits of his neighbors.

Ethan Corder, a homesteader who was one of the first to set up a small farm in the valley about twenty miles east of the mountain that Calhoun called home, rode out in front of the others. Calhoun knew Ethan Corder to be a decent sort, a man of his word, upright and honest. Though Calhoun never could understand a man who chose farming as his livelihood.

The other three men rode a ways back behind Corder, following him because they did not know where they were going.

Those men might not know where they were going, but Moses Calhoun knew well enough. As they cut toward the mountain, Calhoun knew there was only one place they could be going.

Calhoun clicked his tongue at the yellow cur dog with the black mouth.

"C'mon boy," he called. "Let's get home before Kee Kuttai shoots one of these men."

The dog started to follow but then turned back, reluctant to give up some smell he'd found on the ground. Calhoun continued to walk away from the rocky ledge, and as he started up the trail toward his mountain cabin, the dog finally decided to follow.

The ledge was not terribly far from the cabin, not much over a mile, and Calhoun soon came into the small clearing that he called home.

His cabin sat at the edge of a wide meadow, pushed up near a woods of spruce and tall lodgepole pines. In the springtime, the meadow sang with the bright colors of flowers and butterflies, and it provided the grazing that kept his horses and mules healthy.

The woods around the house were cleared of underbrush, and the trees had been thinned out for the construction of the cabin and the smokehouse, the lean-to barn and the rough, timber fence of the paddock.

The cur dog had free roam here, as did Calhoun's young children Daniel and Elijah. Though now the boys might have argued that freedom was a foreign notion, for their mother had set them to their chores in the winter garden. They were there with her, pulling carrots and cutting pumpkin gourds.

Calhoun carried in his folded arms a long flintlock rifle. He called it a Tennessee rifle, though others called it a Poor-Boy because it lacked the fancy adornments of the Lancasters that went to men who collected pelts for Eastern outfits. He now leaned the rifle against the wall of his cabin and stepped to the edge of his front porch, nearer to the garden.

"Men are coming," Calhoun called.

His wife was the daughter of a French-Canadian trapper and an Indian woman. She might have come from the Shoshone or some other, smaller, northern tribe. Kee Kuttai never knew for sure how her mother came to be the wife of the Frenchman. She spoke more French than anything else, though she had plenty of English.

"Qui vient visiter?" she asked.

Moses had no French, except what he'd picked up from his wife. But the words all sounded so rushed to him that he could seldom distinguish any part of it, and he really only recognized simple phrases, and even then, only in context. But he did like the sound of it when she spoke French at him – the up and down cadence of it, almost like a song.

"Ethan Corder is leading some men up through the valley," Calhoun said. "Anyway, I reckon I'd appreciate it if you wouldn't shoot them when they come up."

Kee Kuttai smiled prettily at him.

He counted himself a lucky man. Kee Kuttai wore the largest brown eyes he'd ever seen, soft and loving. On long hunts, his imagination often became overwhelmed with her eyes. But even more than her eyes, she'd endured every winter with him without complaint, and it took a hardy woman to survive winters on this mountain without even a little grievance.

Expecting visitors, and not knowing their purpose, Kee Kuttai hurried the boys along in the garden, and soon they took their baskets inside. Daniel, the older of the boys, toted in his arms a pumpkin that was pert near as big as him.

After some time, the cur dog started barking, and Moses Calhoun heard the approach of the men.

The trail up the mountain was little more than a draw, and it did not come all the way to Calhoun's cabin. The trails leading directly to the cabin were just deer paths. For a hundred yards in any direction, Calhoun always varied his descent away from the cabin so that there was no worn trail that would lead a man directly to his door.

When the riders finally emerged out of the woods and into the clearing near his cabin, they were dismounted and leading their horses and mules.

Ethan Corder stopped when he saw Moses Calhoun sitting under the overhang on his porch. The old cur dog recognized Ethan and went up to him with his tail wagging, sniffed at his leg, and stood still for a scratch behind his ear. As a guard dog, the cur was just middling.

"Afternoon, Mose," Corder called out from across the woods. "Mind if I come up?"

Politeness among neighbors went a long way toward preventing disputes.

The men with Corder had a look about them that Moses Calhoun didn't quite trust. They wore heavy, long coats embellished with fur at the collars and cuffs, and vests and wool trousers and clean shirts.

Moses Calhoun learned long ago that if a man made it this far into the mountains in a clean shirt, he probably couldn't be trusted tote his own load.

"Come on, then," Calhoun said.

Corder stepped forward, leading the other men toward the cabin. Calhoun had no hitching post, so the men all tied their horses onto pine branches and stepped up to the front porch. Ethan Corder relaxed, leaning his shoulder into one of the posts, but the other men stood in front of the porch, stiff and wooden.

Moses Calhoun looked over the men who'd come up with Corder. One of them wore a badge on his vest, half of it visible from behind his coat. The others looked like they might be lawyers or shop owners, and while Moses Calhoun didn't mind doing business with shop owners when he had pelts to sell or needed to buy provisions, but he kept a wide berth of lawyers.

But one of them had a different look. One of the men wore two Colt Dragoons on his belt, one on his thigh and one across his hip, flipped backwards in a cross-draw fashion that most anyone recognized as a gunfighter's rig. The man worked hard to give himself an icy stare, a hard look that suggested he was a hard man.

"Going to be a cold winter," Ethan Corder said conversationally. "Already a cold wind blowing through the valley."

"What brings you up so high, Ethan?"

Corder grinned at Calhoun. The two men were neighbors in a place where neighbors lived twenty miles away, but it wasn't the same as being friends. There was a mutual respect there, because they'd both survived harsh winters. And Calhoun trusted Ethan Corder as an honest man, but trust also did not mean friendship. They'd never once hunted together.

"These gentlemen come up from the town, Moses," Ethan Corder said. He nodded toward one of the men. "This here is Sheriff Wooten, and I reckon I'll let him do his own talking."

Moses Calhoun, wearing buckskin shirt and britches, with a thick beard and casting cold eyes on the strangers, knew townspeople often found him and those like him to be intimidating. Even rugged townspeople, who survived harsh winters in their own way, harbored a suspicious curiosity toward the men who lived isolated in the mountains – trappers and hunters.

"Mr. Calhoun, like Mr. Corder said, my name is Sheriff Michael Wooten. These gentlemen with me, they're all folks I've deputized to ride along with me as a posse."

"I don't reckon I've broken any of your laws. And if I have, I certainly ain't done it in the town," Moses Calhoun interrupted. His tone, purposefully, contained more than a hint of hostility. If the townsfolk harbored suspicions about men like Moses Calhoun, men like Moses Calhoun harbored their own suspicions about townsfolk. Especially those who wore a badge.

"No, sir," Sheriff Wooten chuckled. "I reckon you ain't at that. But we ain't here for you, Mr. Calhoun. You don't have to fear that."

"I ain't afraid," Moses Calhoun said, cutting him short.

The sheriff chuckled again.

"Fact is, we were hoping you might be able to help us," Wooten said.

"Help in what way?"

"As I was saying, we come from down in the town, yonder, and what brought us up here was that we had a murder, back about five days ago."

Calhoun narrowed his eyes at the man, wondering why any of this had anything to do with him.

"We tracked the men who done it west," Wooten said. "Two days ago, three days after the killing, the men rode into Mr. Corder's place down in the valley. They spent a night in his barn, and they bought some provisions off him."

"I didn't know what had happened back at the town," Corder interjected. "I just thought they were traveling through and needed a place to bed down."

Wooten continued, "And Mr. Corder knows the men continued west, down through the valley below."

"I sold 'em some bacon and flour and a pack mule," Ethan Corder said. "Sold them some old tools, too. They lingered some yesterday morning, trying to decide where to go, and asked me all sorts of questions about what might be where if they went one way or t'other. And then I watched 'em ride out through the valley, west of my place and coming along this way."

"We think they're making for the goldfields up in the new territory," Wooten said.

Moses Calhoun didn't know anything about a new territory, but he knew well enough that men from down below had been flocking northwest for the last two or three years because gold had been found in some streams in Idaho Territory.

"Just in conversation, I asked 'em if they were going to the goldfields," Corder explained. "That caught their interest, and they asked how best to get there. So I told 'em if they cut through the valley and made the pass to the west and kept going, they'd strike the Bozeman Trail and that would take them north to Virginia City."

Moses Calhoun once hunted the Valley of the Flowers, many years ago, but found himself unwelcome by the Crow Indians who lived in the area and had never gone back. He knew white men had established a trail through the valley leading to the northern goldfields, and he'd heard it called the Bozeman Trail, even though Moses Calhoun personally knew at least two dozen hunters and trappers who'd used that trail long before Mr. Bozeman came along.

But he'd never heard of Virginia City. The only thing he knew up that way was a little place called Varina, but that was no town, just a small mining camp.

"Varina?"

Wooten chuckled again.

"They're calling it Virginia City now," the sheriff said. "Varina's a Rebel name."

"Is it?" Calhoun asked.

Some years ago, Moses Calhoun had come west from the mountains of North Carolina, and though he knew there was a war going on back east, Calhoun's sympathies along those lines did not extend beyond himself and his small family. He did not know nor care why the Easterners were fighting each other, and he strictly avoided the people who showed an interest in telling him about it.

"They won't make Varina or the Valley of the Flowers, neither, before the snow starts," Moses Calhoun observed. "If they head west or north, they're almost three hundred miles from the nearest settlement."

"And they know they're wanted," Wooten said. "They know – or can guess – that we're out looking for them."

The man with the icy stare stepped forward.

"We reckon they're going to think about finding a hole for the winter," he said. "Find a burrow to get in, pop their heads up in the spring and hope nobody's still hunting for them. Then make for the goldfields early in the spring when there's time in the season left for stomping around in creek beds."

"They've picked a tough place to winter," Moses Calhoun said.

"They're dangerous men, and desperate," Wooten said. "This isn't their first killing, and it isn't their first time roughing it through a winter. They're wanted down in Denver, too. They hid out in the mountains near Denver, winter before last, before making their way up here."

Moses Calhoun took a deep breath, smelling the rich scent of the surrounding fir and spruce trees.

"Well," he said. "I haven't seen nothing of them. You men are the first I've seen pass this way in some while. But I do appreciate you letting me know about them, and I'll be sure to watch out if they come this way."

Wooten glanced at Ethan Corder, and Ethan Corder frowned and shrugged at the man. That look exchanged between them told Moses Calhoun that the men had come for something more than just to provide him with a warning.

"The thing about it is, Mose, these men were hoping maybe you could help them," Corder said.

Calhoun cut him short.

"I cannot," he said.

"We'd pay you to act as a tracker for us," Wooten said. "A dollar a day."

"Plus there's a bounty," the man with the icy stare said. "You'd get thirty dollars for each of the men we bring in, whether they're dead or alive. It's four men we're talking about who are wanted back in Denver. That's one hundred and twenty dollars we'd pay you."

Wooten cut in.

"Four men, plus we think they picked up a fifth in town. There ain't a bounty on him."

Calhoun shook his head.

"I ain't a bounty hunter," he said. "And I ain't a

lawman. I keep to my own, and it serves me fine."

Again, the glance between the two men.

"Thing about it is, Mr. Calhoun, I believe that man they killed in the town was an acquaintance of yourn," Sheriff Wooten said.

Moses Calhoun narrowed his eyes at the man.

"I doubt that," Calhoun said. "I don't know many folks in the town."

"Moses, it was Eli Simmons," Ethan Corder said.

That froze Calhoun's blood.

When Moses Calhoun first came into these mountains after traveling up the Mississippi River to the Missouri and the Missouri as far as he could get, Eli Simmons was the man who took him under his wing. Old Eli got Moses through his first winter in these mountains, taught him to trap and hunt and where to sell his pelts so that he could earn money.

"Eli Simmons wasn't an acquaintance," Calhoun said heavily. "He was a good friend."

Ethan Corder nodded.

"I know he was," Corder said. "And I knew you'd want to know what happened."

Wooten took a step closer and interrupted Corder.

"These men that killed him, they did it so they could take a bag of silver coins off him. What do you figure was in there, Mr. Calhoun? Maybe forty dollars? That's what they killed your friend for. They went to his cabin and killed him for forty dollars. That's the kind of men they are. And that's why we need to find them."

A hawk let out a loud screech and then swooped

down from higher up the mountain, gliding out over the meadow alongside Corder's cabin. Then it dove straight down into the tall grass of the meadow, and a moment later came up with a mouse or some other small animal in its talons.

"What happened to his daughter and the boys?" Calhoun asked.

"Daughter?" Sheriff Wooten said. "We didn't know anything about a daughter. But that explains some things. Some folks who saw them leave town said they thought an Injun woman was with these men. And we found two Injun boys at the cabin."

Moses Calhoun winced at the words. He glanced over his shoulder at the window of his cabin. The shutter sat open just a touch. Calhoun could see his wife, Kee Kuttai, standing in the shadows listening to the men.

"What happened to the boys?" Calhoun asked.

"They didn't speak much English," Wooten said. "Couldn't hardly tell us what happened. We finally found an old half-breed in the town who could speak some Snake language at them, though by then we'd already pieced together most of what happened. But the boys didn't say anything about a woman, and they didn't say anything about Eli Simmons being their grandfather. I don't think they trusted us much, even with the half-breed doing the interpreting."

"So what became of the children?" Calhoun asked again. "The two boys?"

"We give 'em to a Christian family there in town," Wooten said.

"And no sign of the woman?" Calhoun asked.

"No sign," Wooten said. "We were thinking maybe Eli Simmons took a squaw and maybe she was in cahoots with the men that killed him. Like I said, most of this we had to piece together from what people saw. We know four men followed Simmons home and killed him there, because some people saw them. Then, later, when they left town, someone swore it was five men plus an Injun woman. And Mr. Corder said there wasn't no Injun woman with them when they stopped at his place for the night. And they were back to being four men at Corder's place."

Moses Calhoun looked over at Ethan Corder.

"She wasn't with them when they stopped at your place?"

Ethan shook his head.

"I never saw her," Ethan Corder said. "The men slept in the barn, so I reckon it's possible they snuck her in and out when I wasn't around. But I never saw her."

Moses Calhoun sighed heavily. The day was getting late. The men wouldn't be traveling far before they'd have to make camp.

"You're welcome to camp here tonight," Moses told them. "You can set up your tents yonder by that slope and it'll block the wind a little for you."

"Does that mean you're coming with us?" Wooten asked.

"I ain't decided," Calhoun said. "I'll give you an answer come morning."

***

"You can't go with them," Kee Kuttai said in hushed tones when Moses Calhoun walked into the cabin.

Moses took a deep breath.

"Snow's coming. If not tonight, it'll come tomorrow," Calhoun said. "That's going to put four desperate men close to us, possibly stranded for the winter. When they get hungry, or cold enough, they may come looking for a place to stay. I reckon this place is as good as any."

"So if they come, we will handle that then. You don't have to seek trouble."

Calhoun smiled at his wife. It amused him how her English came and went with her moods.

"They killed Eli Simmons," Calhoun said. "And maybe stole his daughter."

"You did your part for her," Kee Kuttai said.

At Old Eli's request, a year ago, Moses Calhoun had gone to the Snake People's winter camp and taken Eli's daughter and her two sons to Eli's home down in the town. He'd been taken prisoner by the soldiers and attacked by the Indians, and he'd made enemies in the effort. But he'd done what Eli asked of him.

"I did my part for her then," Moses Calhoun said. "But she needs someone now. Her husband's killed by soldiers; her father's killed by thieves. Who else is there?"

"Four men are setting up camp outside," Kee Kuttai said. "Let it be them."

Moses Calhoun scoffed.

"I don't reckon those men can get the job done," he said.

"But you can?" Kee Kuttai asked.

Calhoun sniffed and nodded his head.

"You know that I can."

Kee Kuttai turned from him in a huff.

"Fais comme tu veux," she said, and he didn't catch the words but took the meaning well enough.

Kee Kuttai had turned toward the fireplace where a small fire was burning and the dutch oven was simmering a stew for supper.

Moses walked up behind her and wrapped his arms around her. He put his face into her ebony hair and smelled the earthy scent of a woman who harvested from a kitchen garden and cooked over an open fire. His heart swelled with fondness he had for her.

"If it was me killed and you taken, I'd want someone to come for you," Moses Calhoun whispered into her hair. "How can I want that, and not be willing to do it for someone who was such a friend to me?"

Kee Kuttai huffed at him, but she wrapped her hands around the arms holding her.

The boys watched from a corner of the room. Though they did not know it, both boys were learning lessons, the same as they did when they fished for trout in the streams with their father, or went with him on hunts to bring back deer or elk for the smokehouse. Now they learned lessons both about being a man and about being a husband.

Kee Kuttai spun in her husband's arms so that she was facing him.

"Reviens moi vite," she said.

Moses Calhoun nodded. He didn't know the words, but he'd heard them often enough. She uttered the same plea every time he left for a long hunt or when he went below to sell pelts. When he saddled the sorrel horse to ride off to do a favor for a friend, he heard the same words.

He knew what she meant – come back to me soon.

Moses kissed his wife's forehead, and then she ladled stew into four bowls, and the family sat down at their table with two small benches, Moses and the oldest boy, Daniel, on one bench, his wife and the younger boy, Elijah, on the other.

"Won't be long before I have to make another bench, or two," Moses said.

Kee Kuttai put an arm around Elijah and squeezed him close into her side so that the boy made an annoyed face.

"Not yet, though," she said.

- 3 -

Overnight the clouds rolled in and the snow began to fall. Just a light dusting, a taste of what was coming. In the woods, very little snow reached the ground because the canopy of the spruce and lodgepole pines managed to catch all that would stick. But out in the meadow, a crunchy layer of ice and snow rested in patches on the tall grass.

Moses Calhoun was awake before the sun.

He quietly climbed down from the loft in the gable of the small log cabin, trying not to disturb Kee Kuttai or the children. But Kee Kuttai was awake.

She watched her husband from the edge of the loft as he pushed his feet into his boots and shoved the bottoms of his deerskin britches into the top of the boots. He tied the boot tops with leather thongs, not tight enough to make his feet go numb but tight enough to keep out the snow.

He took his pannier from under a cushioned bench and began packing the things he would need. Powder and shot, a couple of extra pair of wool socks, a couple of blankets. He wrapped a belt around his buckskin shirt and put his sheathed Bowie knife down into the belt, and he tied a leather strap onto the belt that he slid his hatchet down into.

The hatchet was a gift from a Snake chief, given to him many years ago. The hatchet was a weapon, and it worked better for fighting off mountain lions than it did for cutting saplings or firewood, but in a tight spot the hatchet could chop kindling.

When his gear was packed, Calhoun hefted the pannier and pushed his way through the door.

Ethan Corder and the other men were camped in two tents they erected in the woods a little ways from the cabin. The first light of dawn was showing against the clouds, and the canvas tents shone white. None of the men were up yet.

Calhoun set the pannier down in the lean-to barn. He took some time to brush both the horse and mule. His sorrel gelding was a sure-footed horse on mountain trails, and he preferred it over the other horses in the paddock. The mule was willing enough, and kept up on long hunts.

By the time he was finished brushing the animals and picking their hooves, the sky was brighter and the light was filtering down into the woods. The men in the tents stirred. Calhoun heard voices. And after a minute or two, Sheriff Wooten came out of one of the tents. He stretched his back and arms and moaned a bit.

Sheriff Wooten appeared to be a man accustomed to sleeping on a mattress.

"Morning," Moses Calhoun said.

Wooten jumped.

"Ha. Didn't see you over there, Mr. Calhoun."

The sheriff tapped the side of his tent.

"Frost," he said. "I can tell you I felt every bit of that cold last night."

"Going to get a lot colder," Calhoun said. "Probably do it fast, too. It's a big wind blowing from the west."

The sheriff turned around like he was looking to the west, but in fact he was facing north.

"Early snow," he said. "It'll be a long winter."

Moses Calhoun nodded.

"It'll be too long," he said. "I need to put more meat in the smokehouse, so if you gentlemen are ready to get moving, we should head out soon."

Wooten sighed heavily and nodded. Moses Calhoun guessed that the sheriff's determination was already wavering. If they couldn't make this a short hunt, Calhoun worried that he'd find himself on his own looking for these four or five men who murdered Eli Simmons.

Wooten slapped his hand against both tents a couple

of times, and then pulled back the flaps.

"Let's get moving," he said. "Daylight is a precious thing."

As the men emerged from their tents, Kee Kuttai and the two children came out of the cabin with five steaming plates of stew and bread and set them on a table on the porch.

"Breakfast for these men," she said, nodding toward the tents but not looking at them. "The sooner you leave, the sooner you will return."

None of the men had seen her the day before, and she was a surprise to all of them, except Ethan Corder who had visited Moses Calhoun in the past and met his wife.

She went back inside without another word.

Wooten and the other men came up to the cabin porch, and each man took up a plate and began eating. The stew was warm, and they were all grateful for it.

The two young boys stayed outside to watch the strangers eat, curious about seeing so many men come to their cabin like this. Over their short lives, many men had stopped by, either on a hunt or traveling to or from town. But never had Daniel and Elijah seen so many men at one time come up to the cabin.

Ethan Corder winked at the boys and made faces at them. A homesteader from down in the valley, Ethan Corder was a family man and had boys of his own. Sheriff Wooten also had children, but they were all grown and living down in Colorado Territory. Wooten came up to the mountains just a couple of years ago, looking to get into the goldfields. But when he arrived in the town down below, he decided he'd gone as far as he cared to go. Someone in town suggested making Wooten sheriff because he'd served as a deputy marshal for a time, and he took the job. His intention was to stay just long enough to make enough money that he could return home to Colorado without embarrassing himself for being gone so long and not earning any money.

But the fact of it was, Sheriff Wooten had a girl he liked to go see in the back room at a saloon in town, and the more he thought about it, the more he dreaded the lectures he knew he would receive from his wife if he went back to Colorado Territory without a single bag of gold. Whether he admitted it or not, Sheriff Wooten was settled, and he'd probably stay sheriff until someone killed him or he up and died on his own.

The man with the icy stare, he paid no heed to the children, and though he ate with as much enthusiasm as the others, he didn't show much appreciation.

Inside the cabin, Moses Calhoun ate his breakfast at the table and watched his wife while she wrapped foodstuffs in cheesecloth for him to take. She was very deliberate with everything she did, taking her time.

A marriage in these mountains was a matter of mutual survival.

For a man's part, he protected and provided. For a woman's part, she tended the garden and prepared the food. Both offered the other some comfort. Warmth in the winter, some companionship to stave off the terrible loneliness. A lot of marriages were unofficial things, and often enough the woman was a slave in an Indian camp and was bought for the price of a broken rifle or a side of meat, and a fair number of the marriages of Calhoun's neighbors were not mutual things. Sometimes a fondness grew between a man and woman, and sometimes a woman traded one unhappy existence for another.

Kee Kuttai, being the daughter of a French-Canadian trapper and his Indian wife, came to Moses Calhoun in an unusual way – by consent. Moses had come to visit a few times, passing through on long hunts. The two had exchanged looks at each other on those occasions. A cold winter took her mother. In the spring her father went on a long hunt, leaving Kee Kuttai and her younger brother alone at the lonely cabin deep in the mountains.

Late in the season, shortly after the first snow, Moses Calhoun found the man at the bottom of the gorge where he'd fallen to his death. His body picked apart by wolves, Calhoun recognized him from his knife. Calhoun went to the cabin and offered to take the young woman and her brother down into a town. The winter caught them, and Kee Kuttai and her brother lived with Moses Calhoun in his small cabin. By the time the snow melt came, she had decided she would stay.

That was years ago now, and two sons, and during that time they built together a life of contentment. Neither of them thought much of love, neither the word nor the notion. Instead, they thought of their marriage in terms of attraction and affection, warmth and comfort, food and clothing, sometimes with laughter and joy. For both of them, their relationship existed as a partnership against the harsh winters, and in this territory, that meant significantly more than an emotion.

But Kee Kuttai had been in these mountains he entire life, and that was long enough to understand the dangers. There were dangers enough for a man going out into the deep wilderness at this time of year, even if he wasn't seeking four killers. The bear would be looking for a last meal before going to their dens. Wolves and lions, too, would want to put on weight before the lean time came. A man's campfire might attract any number of troubles. A misplaced foot on the trail could end in disaster.

And to compound her reasons for worry were the four killers.

"Je n'aime pas que tu partes," she said, wrapping a side of bacon in a cloth.

"What's that?" Moses Calhoun said.

"I do not want you to go with these men," Kee Kuttai said. "Dangereuse."

She used the French pronunciation, but Calhoun knew the meaning well enough.

"I'll take care," he said.

Kee Kuttai walked over to him and pressed her lips against his forehead. She rested a hand on his shoulder, feeling the taut muscle there. She wanted her hand to have the strength to press him down, to keep him from getting up and leaving. Even when he left on hunts, she was nervous that he would not return. Though she knew that if he was to provide for their family, the hunts were as necessary as planting the kitchen garden or smoking meat, or chinking the walls. This, though – this hunt for killers – it had nothing to do with survival.

A woman alone in these mountains had few options, and none of them were any good. If something were to happen to her husband, Kee Kuttai knew the rest of her life would almost surely be one of misery. Even if she could find a way to raise the boys into adulthood and then rely on them, the intervening years would prove to be cruel, and then she would live out the remainder of her life knowing she was a burden on her sons.

She needed her husband to return healthy and whole.

At last, Moses Calhoun stood up and went to the fireplace. He took down his Tennessee rifle, hanging from hooks driven into the rock chimney. The flintlock long gun had served him well on hunts. Some folks called it a "Poor-Boy" because it lacked the brass and steel furniture of the Lancaster rifles that many men in the wilderness carried. Those men acquired those Lancasters by working for outfits that sent men west to seek pelts. They marked themselves as men who took wages for their work, but Moses Calhoun's gun served as a sign to anyone who understood such things that Calhoun was an independent man, beholden to no one, who came to the mountains on his own. Most of those outfits were gone now, finding it easier to buy pelts than employ men, and only the hardiest of those original trappers and hunters still remained.

He put the long gun in a buckskin sheath and set it by the door. In a chest against a wall he had a Colt Navy revolver, a gun he'd taken off a soldier who had once held him prisoner. He had taken to carrying the gun over the summer, more as a precaution against wolves and cats than anything else. But on a hunt for four killers, he reasoned that the revolver might come in handy. He had gone to town back in the spring and bought a box of percussion caps and shot for the revolver.

He stuck his big Bowie knife and his hatchet in his belt. The hatchet, in particular, had proved over the years to be his best fighting tool. The hatchet was a gift from a Snake chief.

Fully armed, Moses Calhoun gave his wife a lingering look.

"I'll think about you while I'm gone," he said.

***

The men walked their horses part of the way along the trail down into the valley from the cabin, but as the slope eased and a natural trail emerged, Moses Calhoun stepped into the stirrup without a word, and the other men followed his lead. Mounted, it did not take them long to wind their way along the switchback trail down to the wide valley below.

In the valley they found that the grass proved stronger than the dusting of snow from overnight. It stood tall with the snow almost like a thin veil caught between the blades of grass so that it didn't even seem to touch the ground. The sky remained overcast with gray, rolling clouds that hung low in the air.

Calhoun sat back in the saddle so that the sorrel knew to come to a stop, and he waited for the other men to circle around him.

"Those are snow clouds if I've ever seen them," Moses Calhoun reported. "We'll want to make quick work of this."

"That's it for me," Ethan Corder said. "I've got chores to see to at home, Moses. I told these men that I would lead them up to your cabin, but I ain't riding along with the posse."

The statement caught Calhoun by surprise, and he chewed his lip for a moment. Ethan Corder was the only one of these men who he knew, and he wasn't aware that Corder was going to leave him with four strangers. But he did not raise an objection, instead offering a hand to Ethan Corder.

"Bon hiver," Moses said, borrowing a phrase he'd learned from his French-speaking wife.

Ethan Corder tipped his head.

"Sorry to leave you like this, Mose, but with snow coming early I've got to see to my livestock."

Calhoun nodded, considering to himself the things he needed to see to. But he'd agreed to join these men, and he wouldn't back out of it now.

With Corder heading home to the east, Calhoun led the other men at a walk out through the valley.

"How far were you able to track these men?" Corder asked sheriff Wooten.

"We tracked them as far as Corder's place," the sheriff said. "He saw them ride west into the valley, but we don't know where they might have got to. Mr. Corder thought that if you hadn't seen them, you might at least be able to reckon out where they would have gone."

"Were they afoot?" Calhoun asked.

"No, sir," Wooten said. "We know they had horses and at least a couple of mules. We did come across a homesteader not far outside of the town who thinks he saw them. If that was them, the woman was with them still, riding one of their mules."

"They've got a day's head start on us," Calhoun said. "If they're headed for the goldfields and plan to try to make Varina, they'll have to cross this valley and head through the pass. Beyond the pass there's another long valley to get through before they could make the Bozeman Trail. Moving fast and assuming no more snow, they wouldn't make the Trail before five days, maybe six or seven if their horses ain't fit."

"They stayed at Corder's place most of the morning yesterday," Sheriff Wooten said. "Probably only had a four or five hour jump on us."

Calhoun nodded.

"I never did see any sign of them yesterday, but it's possible they come up through the valley and I wouldn't have known it."

Calhoun thought about how much farther beyond his cabin four or five men with horses and mules, and maybe a woman, would be able to get. If they were smart, they wouldn't have camped too close to a stream. This time of year, fresh water attracted every predatory animal in the mountains, all of them looking for one last good meal before the snow set in.

"There's a spot about ten miles up ahead where I sometimes stop to make camp if I can't reach home before night," Moses Calhoun said. "You said these men are from the Colorado Territory?"

"Hid out in the mountains outside of Denver once before," Wooten said.

"Like as not, experience has taught them how to recognize a good campsite. We'll ride up that way and see what we can find."

The men traveled on in silence, Calhoun setting a brisker pace than he had in the beginning.

He knew it would prove difficult to catch the men unless they got lost trying to make the pass or a big snow blew in.

"If a snow comes, it could slow these men down,"

Calhoun said, thinking out loud.

"What's that?" Sheriff Wooten asked.

"Snow might slow them down," Calhoun said. "Give us a chance to catch them."

"Snow would slow us down, too," said the man with the icy stare.

Moses Calhoun glanced back at the man. He could not remember if anyone introduced him to the other men in the party. He'd caught Wooten's name, but his interaction with the others had been limited to this point, and if he'd been told their names he'd forgotten them. He didn't know anything about any of them, except Wooten.

"If you boys can keep up with me, the snow won't slow us down," Calhoun said. "If they get lost trying to make the pass, that might allow us to catch them. Or if they're just lazy, we could catch them up. Otherwise, this is just a horse race and they've got a five- or six-hour lead on us, and I reckon we'll never catch them."

The men were riding up pretty close to Calhoun, now, not spread out behind him like before. He gave the icy-stare man an appraising look, probably letting it linger too long. The man dressed in pretty decent clothes, but they were worn clothes, a little threadbare. The others, including the sheriff, wore good clothes, clean and new. But this one, he had a look that suggested he'd done some rough work. The man's icy stare fell on Calhoun and stayed there.

"You know, I didn't catch your name," Calhoun said.

"Nobody throwed it at you," the man said.

The icy stare, the short quips. He was obviously a man who fancied himself to be intimidating.

"Fair enough," Moses said. "What is your name?"

"Henry Chatham," he said, and the way he said it and kind of cocked his head, Moses Calhoun got the distinct impression he was supposed to recognize the name. But it didn't mean anything to him. Most all the names he knew these days were the names of his neighbors.

"What's your line, Mr. Chatham?"

"Similar to you," Chatham said.

Moses Calhoun chuckled a bit.

"Is that right?"

"Similar," Chatham said. "Not exact. I go looking for men who have a bounty on them."

Calhoun chewed his lip, wondering.

"Is that a Southern accent I detect?" he asked.

"I'm from Alabama," Chatham said. "If you're wondering, I'll own it. Before the war started, I mostly hunted fugitive slaves. Now I hunt fugitive outlaws."

The men rode on through the valley. All of them lost track of time as they went. It seemed slow going, until they picked up their heads and looked along the backtrail and got a sense of how far they'd come. And then, after a long while, Calhoun touched a leg to his horse's side, and the sorrel veered off toward the spruce forest. The mountains lining the valley were covered in thick forests of spruce and lodgepole pines, fir trees, and sometimes a grove of aspen. In places, those thick forests seemed to spill down from the mountains and stretch into the valley, and it was into one of these places that Calhoun directed his horse.

He ducked a branch and rode into the forest.

None of the other men saw anything resembling a
trail, but Calhoun – or the sorrel – seemed to know the
way. The followed a rising ridge a ways up the side of the
mountain, and then came to a place that none of the men
had noticed from down below. It was a great ledge,
jutting up out of the tops of the trees, with a rock face
dropping twenty or twenty-five feet straight down. At the
back of the ledge, the mountain rose sharply, and the cliff
face curved so that the ledge was protected by the cliff
from two sides, the north and west, and protected from
the steep drop to the south. The only way to access the
ledge was from the east. A few trees on the large ledge
provided a little bit of shelter and cover so that it was not
immediately noticeable from below.

"If they're any kind of mountain men, they'd have
seen this ledge and realized it presented a prime spot to
camp, especially for men on the run," Calhoun said.

The ledge was plenty large enough to hold men and
their horses, and they'd only be seen from below if they
built up a fire big enough to put off smoke.

"It's a bit windy up here," Sheriff Wooten noted. "It's
a cold wind, too. I would think they'd prefer to camp in
the woods where there's more of a break from that
wind."

Calhoun shrugged.

"Wind might be cold, but it's not going to eat you like
a bear might," he said. "Out here, there's only one way a
bear or a mountain lion is going to get at you, and it's
coming right along through here. Not even a mountain
lion could come down that cliff face. You're protected on
three sides. A man who chooses to camp where he can
get out of the wind is a man who wakes up with his leg
gnawed off."

One of the other men chuckled.

Calhoun didn't ride directly out onto the ledge. Instead, he slowed his horse to a halt and then swung a leg over the saddle.

"Let's see if they camped here or might be missing a leg."

Wooten and Chatham followed him out onto the ledge, but the other two men stayed back with the horses and mules.

"Look here," Calhoun said, pointing right away to what at first looked to be just a pile of cut spruce boughs.

"What is it?" Chatham asked.

"Someone has been here recently and built a shelter," Moses Calhoun said. He walked over to the pile of branches and lifted a chopped end. He could see the moist sap. "Fresh cut. Someone camped here not more than two days ago, I'd reckon. But probably last night."

"Here's another," Wooten said, standing back behind a fir tree that hid their view of the other pile of branches. Moses Calhoun walked around and examined the other pile, lifting up the branch that he figured had served as the main beam, and finding the other branches lifted with it before falling away. He easily found a spot where a fire had been made, just a small fire only large enough to cook on. The men had forgone the luxury of a fire for warmth, and that suggested they were cautious men who knew a thing or two. They'd dug a hole for the fire down to the rocky base of the ledge and then covered it back over with dirt, maybe to hide their tracks but more likely just to extinguish the coals. He kicked the dirt out of the hole to expose the fire, and found buried with it some bones of a couple of rabbits.

"Two shelters," Calhoun said. "Judging from the size of them, they could have held two or three people each. The cooked a rabbit, but I don't see evidence that they cleaned it here. Probably shot it down in the meadow and then brought it here with them to cook."

Chatham watched Calhoun, listening to him and paying attention to how he uncovered the story the campsite had to tell. He'd done similar things plenty of times, but he recognized a knowledgeable man when he saw one.

"So you think they stayed here last night," Wooten said.

"Someone did," Calhoun said. "Last night or night before last. But probably last night. And I don't reckon there's that many other people wandering around down in that valley right now."

"So we're on their trail," Chatham said impatiently. "But unless they've stacked a cairn in the shape of an arrow pointing which way they gone, we're wasting time. They've been here. They ain't here now. Let's keep moving."

Calhoun nodded to him.

"Let's keep moving," he agreed.

The men returned to their horses, though Moses Calhoun was not quick to get back into the saddle. He walked around a bit, examining the ground.

"You looking for that stack of rocks?" Wooten asked with a laugh.

"I'm looking for anything that might suggest they went up the slope instead of back down to the valley," he said. "We've found a trace of them, it would be a shame to ride off in the wrong direction now."

The ground was so covered in pine straw, that Calhoun could not readily find a track anywhere, but as he walked a little ways, he saw a small branch of a pine tree that was broken but still hanging. He recognized the branch and understood the story it told because he'd seen it a hundred times. A horse walking through the forest takes a bite at a branch, pulls it, the branch breaks and hangs the way it was being pulled. This one was hanging toward the valley.

"They went back down the slope," Calhoun said.

Chatham didn't wait. He pulled the reins on his horse and started back down the trail toward the valley. The other men followed. Calhoun walked over to the sorrel and stepped into the stirrup. He took up the lead rope of his mule that was wrapped a turn around the saddle horn and gave the mule a tug, starting back down the mountain behind the other men.

- 4 -

Late in the afternoon the dark clouds hovering overhead finally gave up and began spilling their contents. It came down as icy sleet initially, bouncing off the brim of Calhoun's hat, off the head and neck of his sorrel horse. But then snow fell with the sleet, large flakes. The moisture seemed to cool the air around them. Moses Calhoun pulled his buckskin shirt at the collar and gripped it closed.

The men riding with him had a similar response. They also dropped back, riding behind Calhoun in a line that extended a dozen yards.

The sleet gave up, and all that fell now was thick flakes of heavy snow. The flakes landed on the tall grass in the meadow and held fast, clinging together until soon the grass began to bend with the weight. Ahead, valley became like a tunnel, suddenly feeling close and narrow. The falling snow had a way of making a man dizzy, making him feel isolated.

"Should we make a camp?" one of the men from the town called up ahead.

Moses Calhoun glanced back at the man. Already the snow was beginning to collect on the brims of everyone's hats, collect on the shoulders and arms.

"Too much daylight to stop now," Calhoun called back to him.

They trudged on. The snow so far made no difference to their rate of travel. All the men felt the cold of it, though the temperature was not significantly altered, the snow gave a worsening impression of cold. But they still moved on at a good walk. The sorrel gelding seemed indifferent to the change in the weather. But as they went, Calhoun could see the snow building in the meadow. This was no dusting like the snows that had already come over the past couple of weeks, leaving patches clinging to the ground in shady places. It would be the real thing, the serious first snow of winter, and it looked like it might be a good one.

If he was home now, Moses Calhoun would be out at the wood pile splitting kindling, probably bringing an extra few arm loads of wood to put under the overhang on the front porch. Stacked against the house like that, the wood stayed dry and spared Moses – or like as not, Daniel and Elijah – from the labor of walking out to the wood pile to collect more wood for the fire. The boys would be loving it, running in the meadow and sticking out their tongues to catch the big flakes. The cur dog would be chasing after them. Kee Kuttai would pull her blanket around her shoulders and press herself against him, receiving in return an arm around her shoulders and a squeeze.

Calhoun grunted to himself and the sorrel horse snorted back at him.

With the boys at the cabin, the first big snow would be a frolic, and he regretted being here in this valley with these men, two of whom he still didn't even know their names.

But he thought of Eli Simmons, and his daughter Aka Ne'ai – widowed a year ago, orphaned and taken hostage by ruffians. In this territory, a woman like Aka Ne'ai didn't stand a chance without a man to stand up for her, and she'd lost all the men she'd had.

The sorrel seemed to sense Calhoun's thoughts, and the horse picked up the pace. The mule, stubborn enough most of the time, didn't argue with the brisker pace. Soon Calhoun was well ahead of the other men.

They made camp in the shelter of a forest. The other men put up their tents, but Calhoun cut fir and spruce branches and weaved them together to make walls for a small lean-to shelter. He cut larger branches to give the shelter support. Even in the forest the snow was making its way through the canopy, beginning to pile up in patches, but most spots were still bare pine straw with spots of grass finding its way through.

The sorrel horse and mule grazed while Moses built his shelter. Calhoun did not bother with picketing them, not yet. They wouldn't wander far.

"You could share a tent with us," Sheriff Wooten said, walking over to where Moses was working on the shelter.

"This is what I'm accustomed to," he said.

"How bad will it be trying to make our way through the snow tomorrow?" Wooten asked.

Calhoun gave him a look.

"I reckon not too bad," he said. "This ain't your first winter here, though. You know how it gets."

Wooten shrugged.

"I'd say I never did stray much from the town in winter," he said. "I couldn't judge what that valley might be like, or the mountain, neither."

"First snow probably won't make it impassable," Calhoun said. "The pass could get closed off to us, but only if this keeps going for several days. It could stop, and a sunny afternoon might even melt most of it off."

Calhoun looked up through the branches of the tall pines and spruce trees as if the sky might reveal what it intended to do.

"Hard to say what will happen. It's an early snow, that's for sure. Wouldn't be no surprise if this lets up and the days turn warm again."

Wooten took a heavy breath.

"I'd hate to find myself stranded," he said.

"I reckon that's true enough for all of us," Moses said.

Calhoun showed the men had to make a small fire down in a hole, digging out a little tunnel so that air could get in to provide oxygen to the flames.

"It won't keep you warm, but you can cook your food on it," Calhoun explained to them. "A small fire like this won't put off so much smoke that you're likely to attract bear or cougar, and it won't be easy to see if there are Indians about. If we were closer to where they make their winter camps, I guess I'd say we should've cooked our suppers somewhere else and then gone a couple of miles before making camp. But we should be all right tonight."

One of the men from town chuckled.

"I wouldn't think there'd be any Injuns about," he said. "Didn't the soldiers clean them out of this country last winter?"

Calhoun studied the man for a moment. He was a younger man, probably eager for the adventure a posse promised. He wore a thin mustache and had a few black whiskers on his chin, but his cheeks were fresh. Most men in this country, even the ones in town, were older and a little more rough looking than this one, and studying him for the first time, Calhoun was surprised to realize just how young he appeared.

"What did you say your name is, son?" Calhoun asked.

"Paul Bentsen," the boy said.

"How long have you been in these parts?"

"About five years. My pa brought me and my brothers here from Minnesota Territory."

"You live in the town?" Moses asked.

"That's right. My pa has a supply store in town," Paul Bentsen said.

Calhoun nodded.

"I reckon you're accustomed to cold winters, coming from Minnesota," Calhoun said.

"It gets right cold," Bentsen said.

Moses Calhoun stood up and walked over to where he'd set up his shelter and started to make his own fire.

That was ample conversation for him. He sometimes went days with considerably less, and he preferred that. He didn't like Paul Bentsen's crack about the massacre at the winter camp the year before, but he refrained from saying anything about it. He knew how the white folks in the settlements felt about the Indians. For a long time they'd lost property and sometimes lives to Indian raids, some of which had been brutal, and the massacre at the winter camp was cause for celebration among the settlers.

He ate his supper removed from the others. When he was finished with it, he gathered up the mule and the sorrel horse and picketed them on short leads not far from his shelter. Around the time dusk gave up and dark settled in, Calhoun smothered his fire and crawled into his shelter.

Sheriff Wooten arranged the watch that night and said Calhoun could sleep, but the mountain hunter didn't trust these men to keep him alive in this country. He intended to sleep light and be ready if the sorrel horse spooked at some danger.

The shelter did a reasonable job of collecting and holding onto the heat from the fire, and it did a superb job of keeping the wind off him. He bundled himself in his bearskin coat, a heavy coat that kept him warm through the coldest winters. He slept on a blanket on a bed of pine straw and pulled another blanket over himself. At home, sleeping in the loft in the cabin where the warm air from the fire collected, he might even be too hot. Many nights, even in the winter, they left the shutters of the window open and rolled up the bearskin cover to allow some of the heat to escape because the cabin got too warm.

On nights like this, huddled under a blanket and wrapped in his heavy coat, Moses Calhoun dreamed of sleeping in his loft at home.

***

The gelding stayed quiet through the night, but what woke Moses Calhoun was a long, lonely howl of a wolf somewhere in the valley.

Whatever warmth his shelter held onto from his small campfire was now gone. Calhoun had pulled the blanket up over his head, but even cocooned inside the blanket he still felt the cold night clawing at him. He opened his eyes and everything was dark.

With some reluctance, he slid the blanket down from his head and looked out the hole of the shelter. A bit of light was seeping in from the sky above, gray and cold. There was more snow on the ground now, the patches where the snow fell through the canopy of trees were bigger. Calhoun slid himself slowly out of the shelter, hating to leave the little bit of warmth he had there.

A man sat on the ground, leaning against the trunk of a pine, so thoroughly bundled in a blanket that Calhoun wasn't sure which one it was.

"Morning," Calhoun said in greeting, but the watchman didn't respond and Calhoun realized the man was asleep.

"So much for the night watch," he muttered to himself.

He walked out toward the edge of the wood where they had camped to look into the valley. There was not much to see because the first light of dawn offered little light to see by, but it was plain enough that the snow was still falling and had fallen through the night. In the dim light, the meadow shone white with its own blanket. Just a couple of inches. Nothing that would slow the horses or prevent them from moving on in pursuit of the men.

It didn't do any good to think too much about the cold, but Moses Calhoun couldn't help but feel the pain in his half-frozen toes.

To forget about it, he thought of all the times he'd felt frozen toes while camping with Eli Simmons. Old Eli had been a good partner in long hunts. The two men would go off into the mountains together in the late autumn, planning to hunt for two or three weeks. They'd camp together at night and then split up during the day, often covering many miles to get separate from each other so one man's hunt wouldn't disturb the other's.

Friendship was a commodity in these mountains, and ever since Eli gave it up and went down to the town, Moses had missed his company. In recent years, they'd done less hunting together, even when Eli was still making his way as a trapper. Old Eli couldn't keep up and didn't want to slow Moses down.

But even then, it wasn't uncommon for Eli to wander into Calhoun's camp, unexpected, take a seat and share a meal.

So it was that Moses Calhoun's thoughts were of Eli Simmons when the sudden boom of a rifle echoed out across the valley, startling Moses Calhoun and making the sleeping man who was supposed to be keeping watch stir awake.

The shot couldn't have come from more than a couple of miles away.

Calhoun did not waste time. He hurried to his shelter and slid his Tennessee rifle out of the shelter, tossing its sheath back in with his saddle. He grabbed his hatchet and sheathed knife, too, tucking each one into his belt, and pulled out his possibles bag with the powder horn strapped to it.

"What was that? A shot?" Henry Chatham asked, coming out from under his blankets and standing up in front of the pine tree he'd been sleeping against.

"It was," Calhoun said, not wasting time.

Calhoun started back the way he'd come, back toward the edge of the woods.

"Where are you going?" Chatham asked.

"To find out who fired that shot," Calhoun said.

And then he was gone, at a run, through the woods out to the edge of the forest. The snow was shallower there at the edge where the branches had grabbed and held the snow, and Moses Calhoun now ran at the edge of the forest where the snow would not slow him down.

His breathing stayed level in spite of the cold air that chilled his lungs. He knew, even in the cold air, he could manage to lope a mile or a little farther. He carried the long gun in one hand, and that, along with the possibles bag flapping against him, slowed his run, but Calhoun moved quickly along the edge of the wood, not slowing or breaking stride to duck below branches or hop fallen trees.

Moses Calhoun was in his element. He'd plenty of times run after a wounded elk or mule deer to be sure he knew where it fell. More than a few times he'd heard wolves and had to run to be sure his horse and mule were safe after having left them to track game.

But after a few minutes of running, Calhoun found he couldn't keep his breath, and he slowed his pace. The cold air was like icy pins in his chest.

The shot had come from somewhere to the west, deeper into the valley. He judged it to be less than two miles away, and he figured he'd already managed to run half a mile. Even as he ran, the gray light of morning grew to expose the valley all gray and white. They heavy flakes still fell at such a rate that it obscured vision for any distance. Still, Calhoun was certain he was not yet far enough to have reached the location of the gunshot.

Though his muscles hardly felt used, Calhoun found he could not even keep up a jog, and he stopped his run, dropping to a knee below a tall lodgepole pine and breathing heavily to try to catch his breath.

He glanced over his shoulder to see that Henry Chatham was following him, but still at some distance behind, and only just visible in the cascade of snow.

Calhoun stood up straight and kept walking. The chilly air hurt his teeth as he tried, still, to catch his breath. It stung his eyes, and his nose felt frozen shut. But he kept moving, kept going deeper into the valley.

And then, some distance ahead, Calhoun caught sight of a small mass of unnatural darkness in the meadow – maybe two hundred yards ahead of him and out in the meadow, away from the forest.

In the gray light and falling snow, the mass might

have been nothing more than a bush or a tree, but Moses Calhoun recognized it for what it was. A group of mounted men. He couldn't make their numbers. Maybe four or five, plus a couple of spare pack mules. And they were not moving. They'd not seen him, but they appeared to be stopped, waiting for something.

Calhoun searched the meadow nearer, and he saw it. A man by himself, out in the meadow, bent down over something.

Quick enough, Moses Calhoun understood what he saw. Whether simply for sport or maybe meat, the riders had seen some animal, and one among their number had fired a shot and struck his target. He'd dismounted and walked back to examine his kill.

Calhoun stepped behind the cover of the trees to keep from being seen, and he motioned for Chatham to make the rest of his journey through the woods.

In a few moments, the man caught up to him.

"What is it, Calhoun?"

"Riders ahead. Four, maybe five of them. And a man out in the meadow there, not a hundred yards from us."

Moses Calhoun pointed out to the man what he'd seen.

"Is that them?" Chatham asked.

"It's someone," Calhoun said. "I couldn't say who."

- 5 -

"What do we do?" Chatham asked, huddling tight inside his clothes.

Calhoun took a glance at the man. He'd grabbed his gunbelt and had both revolvers strapped around him, but he was right now buttoning his heavy coat, and that was going to make those guns difficult to get at. As they stood there, Calhoun rammed a ball down the barrel of his long rifle and poured powder into the pan.

"If you're going to button that, I'd put one of those guns in your hand," Calhoun said.

Chatham narrowed his eyes and pursed his lips, as if Calhoun was telling him something he did not already know.

"Here's what we're going to do," Calhoun said. "You make your way down toward them others. Stay inside the edge of the tree line so that they don't see you coming. I'm going to walk out there and introduce myself."

"Just walk up to him?" Chatham asked.

"Why not?" Calhoun said. "That's what I'd do if I came upon a man hunting under any other circumstances."

"What if he pulls a gun on you?" Chatham asked.

"Then I reckon I'll wish he's a poor shot," Calhoun said.

What Calhoun did not say was that the man had just shot an animal, and he'd probably not taken time to load his rifle after the shot. He was out in the meadow, in the snow, and likely believed he was alone. So if he had a six-shooter, it was doubtful he had it on his person. Calhoun didn't think much about going out to see the man.

While Chatham started to make his way under the cover of the trees, Calhoun stepped out from behind the trees into the wide valley meadow. He felt the big flakes of snow blowing under his hat to land on his cheeks and nose. The air whipped cold, and Calhoun's face felt frozen. In the dim light and the pouring snow, he doubted the others would see him until he was nearly out to the other man. He held his long gun casually across his folded arms, but his muscles were awake and poised to spin the gun and make a shot.

Calhoun closed the distance, feeling the tension in

his body. He knew there was risk in this.

The light breeze and the wet sound of the falling snow masked his footfalls as he crunched through the snow closer to the man until he was just a few feet away. Then everything happened.

The riders up ahead spotted Calhoun. He heard a muffled shout – a warning to the man bending over a fallen elk. The man heard it, too, but he looked back to his party without noticing the man walking toward him through the snow.

The others began to ride, leaving their partner. He shouted to them, but of course they could not hear him any more than he could hear them.

Then he looked around, bewildered, and caught sight of Moses Calhoun, now quickening his pace to close the distance.

"Who the hell are you?" the man demanded.

"My name's Calhoun. I live not far from here. Heard the shot, and was curious to know who was about in this weather."

The bewilderment did not leave the man's face. He looked back to where the others had been just a few moments ago, but now they were invisible, gone beyond what the man could see in the gray light and falling snow.

"Who are you?" the man said, leaning toward Calhoun.

"That's what I asked you," Moses Calhoun said, still taking steps toward the man.

They were now nearly face-to-face, and Calhoun had a better look at him. He did indeed have a six-shooter strapped to his hip, but his heavy wool coat hung down over it so that the man wouldn't be able to get to it in a hurry if he decided to make a try.

The man frowned, still trying to make sense of being approached in a snow storm in a remote valley.

"Where'd you come from?" he asked.

"I come from back yonder," Calhoun said, tossing his head behind him.

Now he was up to within reach of the man.

Calhoun nodded down toward the elk.

"That's a good kill," Calhoun said.

The man looked down at the animal, and Calhoun moved fast. He swung the Tennessee rifle so that it was pointing forward at the stranger, and in seamless motion, Calhoun jabbed it forward and hit the man in the chest. It wasn't a powerful punch, but he stumbled back, and with the snow and the elk's legs tripping him, he fell over backwards.

The man landed with his arms outstretched, and he whined up at Calhoun.

"What the hell did you do that for?" he asked.

Calhoun pointed the rifle at the man.

"Because that man you killed back in town was a friend of mine," Calhoun said.

The stranger started to make for his gun, but Calhoun cocked back the flintlock.

"You make for that weapon on your belt, and I'll put a hole in you big as this valley," Calhoun said.

Over his shoulder, Calhoun heard a man running toward them, breathing heavy.

"They rode off," Chatham called.

"I saw," Calhoun said. He waited until Chatham was closer, then asked, "Is this one of 'em?"

Chatham jogged the last few yards to where Moses was standing. He bent almost double and dropped his hands to his knees, his shoulders moving with every big breath he drew.

He studied the man on the ground and nodded his head a few times.

"Yep. Wesley Mullen."

"Don't walk in front of my gun," Calhoun said. "But reach down there and take his gun and that knife on his belt. Let's get him back to Sheriff Wooten."

Chatham took one last big gulp of air and then nodded his head. He stepped wide around the man on the ground and then bent beside him to remove the weapons. As he did, he kneeled down and put his knee right on Wesley Mullen's wrist so that the man couldn't make a move with it if he wanted.

Calhoun noted it. Chatham knew his business. He knew how to take a prisoner and render him all but harmless.

After he disarmed the man, Chatham groped Wesley Mullen by the back of his collar and dragged him to a standing position. Calhoun kept the rifle on him, but he lowered the hammer to a half-cock position.

"My name ain't Wesley Mullen," he said as Chatham began to push him forward. His defense was weak.

"I know you, Mullen," Chatham said. "I've been coming after you all the way back since Denver."

Mullen had nothing else to say after that.

Chatham directed Mullen back toward the edge of the tree line, and Calhoun followed them. He kept his neck on a swivel, watching their back trail to be sure Mullen's friends did not turn around and try to make a rescue. But as the gray light filled the snowy meadow and exposed the mountains beyond the valley with their fresh white blankets, Calhoun saw no sign of the riders who had abandoned their friend.

***

Sheriff Wooten and the other two were awake and stirring about the camp when Calhoun and Chatham returned with their prisoner. Calhoun could smell their campfire through the wet snow and fresh pine air long before the campsite came into view.

Chatham made a short explanation of how they'd come to have a prisoner, and Wooten put a pair of iron handcuffs on Wesley Mullen.

"Should we mount and get after them others?" Paul Bentsen asked, eager to be finished with this chore and get on back home where there was a fire in the fireplace and snow wasn't piling on the brim of his hat.

Sheriff Wooten took a deep breath, and Moses Calhoun could see from the man's face that he had something to say.

"Look here, Mr. Chatham," Sheriff Wooten said. "I'm going to take this prisoner back to town. The rest of you men keep tracking the others."

Bentsen and the other man – Calhoun still had not figured out his name – both gaped at the sheriff, but neither Chatham nor Moses Calhoun were much surprised with this decision.

"We can't be riding after these men with a prisoner," Wooten said. "And the fact is, I've got too much to do back home to keep going."

The other one, the one without a name, interrupted.

"Sheriff, I've got to get back to my store. Every day I'm out here, I'm losing my livelihood. Why don't you let me take the prisoner back?"

Wooten scoffed.

"Irwin, this man is a dangerous killer," Wooten said. "I can't let you take him back to town by yourself."

The man Wooten called Irwin began to bicker, and Moses Calhoun walked away from the four men debating what they intended to do.

The prisoner, Wesley Mullen, stood leaning against a tree, his arms twisted behind his back and his wrists in iron.

Moses Calhoun walked up close to the man and spoke in a low tone.

"The Indian woman you took from the cabin in the town," he said. "Is she with your party."

Wesley Mullen looked away without providing an answer.

Calhoun took a breath.

"You see those men over there?" Calhoun said. "Bickering like a bunch of elk bucks on the rut. They want to take you back to a judge and hang you so they can get paid for it. But I ain't with them. I'm here to fetch that woman because she's the daughter of my friend. My friend you killed."

Calhoun slid his Bowie knife from its sheath in his belt and took Wesley Mullen's earlobe between his finger and thumb, giving it a tug to pull it taut from his head.

"Ow," Mullen complained.

Calhoun growled at the man.

"You smirk and don't answer my question, and the judge won't have enough pieces of you to hang from a rope," Calhoun said.

He took a swift swipe up with the knife, slicing the earlobe straight off. Mullen yelped. Immediately the ear began to pour blood down the side of the man's neck. Calhoun dangled the severed lobe in front of the man's face and then tossed it onto the ground.

"Is the Indian woman still with those men?"

"Damn you!" Wesley Mullen shouted. "You cut my ear off!"

Wooten and the others looked around for the sudden commotion, and the sheriff started toward Calhoun and the prisoner.

"Answer my question, or I keep cutting until your scalp comes loose," Calhoun said.

"Mr. Calhoun," Wooten said, stepping over to intervene. But Moses Calhoun turned on the sheriff.

"This ain't your affair, Sheriff Wooten. You go on back to your conversation and you men decide what you're going to do. Mr. Mullen and I are having our own conversation."

Wooten started to say something, but Mullen cut him off.

"The man is a maniac," he cried. "Get him off of me!"

Mullen started to try to get away, but Calhoun kicked his legs out from under him, and Mullen went face first into a thick patch of snow. He rolled away onto his back, and the snow where his ear had hit was red with blood.

Calhoun planted his knee in the man's chest, leaning all his weight down on it so that Mullen could barely breathe.

"The woman, is she still with those men or not?" Calhoun asked.

Mullen glanced around, but he was getting no more help from Sheriff Wooten. For his part, the sheriff wasn't sure if it was safe to intervene. His suspicions of mountain people were being proved out, and he did not want to get caught in the middle. Wesley Mullen looked ready to cry.

"She's with them," he said, whimpering.

"But the man whose barn you slept in never saw her," Calhoun said. "If she's with them, why didn't he see her?"

Mullen frowned. Moses Calhoun wanted to press the issue with him, force him into the truth. It mattered, Calhoun knew, if Aka Ne'ai – Eli Simmons' daughter – was alive and with the others of Mullen's party. It would dictate how he went forward.

"We hid her in the woods," Mullen said. "We tied her in the woods so she wouldn't be seen. When we rode out of there, we went and fetched her."

Calhoun nodded.

"How many?" he asked.

"How many what?"

"How many men are there?" he said, driving his knee a little harder into Mullen's chest. "If you need me to slice off a couple of your fingers to help you count 'em, I can do that."

"Get this maniac off of me!" Mullen shouted.

Henry Chatham had come over to scene of violence and was watching with amused interest. Wooten's disgust had made him walk away, and Bentsen and Irwin were both standing with the sheriff.

"Nobody's going to help you," Henry Chatham said. "You may as well answer his questions."

Calhoun let up with his knee, and he handled Mullen roughly, rolling the man onto his stomach and then gripping at his fingers. Mullen clenched both hands into fists, and Calhoun nearly broke his fingers prying them loose.

"There's four more, plus the woman," he blurted out in a panic. "For God's sake, don't chop my fingers!"

"Four more?" Calhoun said.

"That's it," Mullen answered. "Four, plus the woman."

"What are they going to do with the woman?" Calhoun asked.

"What do you think?" Mullen cried at him.

Calhoun pressed the Bowie knife against the man's thumb, right at the joint, until blood showed.

"They're looking to sell her," Mullen shouted. "For God's sake, don't cut my thumb off!"

"Sell her to who?" Calhoun asked.

"Whoever they can find."

Henry Chatham walked over and put his boot on Mullen's cheek, pressing the man's head hard into the ground.

"Who's the fifth man with your outfit, Mullen?" he asked. "I know your brother Harlan is leading your gang. And Buddy Carver and Slap Duncan. But who's the fifth man?"

"Just some guide we picked up in town," Mullen said. "Bearclaw somebody."

"Bearclaw Jim?" Calhoun asked. "Missing a finger and a thumb on his right hand?"

Mullen sounded surprised.

"Yeah, that's right. That's him."

Chatham narrowed his eyes at Moses Calhoun.

"You know the man?"

Calhoun nodded his head one quick time.

"I know Bearclaw Jim," he said. "I'm the one who removed the finger and thumb."

Calhoun stepped away from the prisoner. He had the answers he wanted, and more.

He turned toward Wooten. His posture suggested a purposeful challenge to the sheriff, inviting him – daring him – to offer complaint about the treatment Calhoun had given to the prisoner. But Sheriff Wooten balked. Whether he was thoroughly frightened by Calhoun or just simply wanted to avoid a confrontation, the sheriff instead went back to his debate with the other men about which one of them would take the prisoner back to town.

Moses Calhoun ducked down into his shelter and slid out his gear and started packing it. There wasn't much to it, and in a few minutes, he had the pannier on the mule and the horse saddled.

All the while, the other men argued with each other, and finally Chatham walked away in a huff.

That's when Wooten came over to Calhoun.

"Irwin and I are riding back with the prisoner," Wooten said. And then he waited. He did not know Moses Calhoun, didn't know how the man would take this information. Wooten, like men who carry some sort of authority granted by the government sometimes will, carried an inflated sense of his own importance. He'd come to believe that Moses Calhoun was riding along with this posse out of a respect for the badge on Wooten's chest, and he did not understand the real reason that Moses Calhoun was in this valley, guiding these men.

Calhoun offered no response.

After a silence that grew uncomfortable, Wooten said, "Will you continue to help Mr. Chatham track these men?"

Calhoun chewed his lip for a moment.

"Sheriff, I'm going after these men. If you or Chatham or anyone else cares to follow me, I won't make an effort to stop you."

Sensing his authority was somehow being undermined, Sheriff Wooten tried to snatch some of it back.

"Well, the offer for a dollar a day stands," he said. "My office will pay that to you. As for the bounty, that's something you'll have to take up with Chatham. The bounty is being offered out of Denver, and that doesn't have anything to do with me."

Calhoun slid his sheathed rifle into the straps of his saddle, and then he stepped into the stirrup.

"You tell Mr. Chatham and Mr. Bentsen, if they want to follow me, they need to get moving," Moses said. "I'm riding on now."

With that, Calhoun touched the horse's side with his leg and the sorrel horse took a couple of reluctant steps, still trying to wake up and warm up. Calhoun gave a tug to the lead rope, and the mule followed. He turned the mule's lead once around his saddle horn. If the mule spooked and bolted or turned stubborn and bucked at going farther, the rope would come loose easy enough. But this was probably unnecessary precaution – the mule wasn't given to ornery behavior.

Calhoun ducked branches to get out of the woods, riding past Chatham and Bentsen, Wooten and Irwin, and the prisoner and his bleeding ear.

"Calhoun, where the devil are you going?" Chatham demanded. "Our horses aren't even saddled yet."

But Moses Calhoun did not pay the man any attention. The sorrel gelding, sensing Calhoun's desire to move fast, gave a good walk, and the mule did not object. It did the animals good, in the cold, to move with purpose and keep the blood flowing.

- 6 -

Bearclaw Jim still felt the terrible ache in his hand a year later. The cold made it worse, it seemed.

When he saw the man come out of the darkness beyond the falling snow and approach Wesley Mullen, Jim was the one who called for the rest of the party to skedaddle.

Harlan Mullen didn't care much to leave his little brother, but he also didn't care much to get his neck stretched at the end of a rope. Bearclaw Jim led them to the cusp of the woods where the snow was not yet quite as a deep and they could run the horses a little faster.

After some time, when they'd covered ample distance, Bearclaw Jim slowed his horse.

The slower pace gave Harlan Mullen a chance to catch up. He was pulling the Indian woman on a mule. The mule possessed an uncooperative streak and had made the trip so far a true burden for Harlan Mullen.

"Damn mule," he said. "No wonder that farmer sold us the mule."

Bearclaw Jim looked back over his shoulder, but he wasn't looking at Harlan Mullen. Instead, he was looking deep into the valley, the way they'd just ridden, to see if anyone was in pursuit.

"What happened back there?" Harlan Mullen asked. "What was that?"

Bearclaw Jim laughed a wheezy laugh until he began to cough. When he got his composure back, he said, "We abandoned your brother is what happened."

The man wore a grin and showed several missing teeth. He seemed to take great pleasure in leaving someone behind, and Harlan failed to understand why.

"Who was that?" Mullen repeated.

Bearclaw Jim looked at the stump on his hand where his thumb and forefinger used to be – shot away a year ago when he was working as a guide for the soldiers.

"I think I might know," Bearclaw Jim said. "I might be wrong, but I think I know."

Harlan Mullen shrugged.

"Did he take Wesley?" he asked.

"It looked that way," Bearclaw Jim said. "Why else

would he knock him down like that?"

They'd seen the stranger walk up to Wesley, and Harlan Mullen had shouted a warning to his brother. But the snow and breeze and distanced muffled the warning. They saw the man use his long rifle to knock Wesley backwards, and that's when Bearclaw Jim started to ride, without warning to the others.

Scared, the others followed.

Harlan Mullen was the older brother by eight years. There were three siblings – two sisters and a brother – between Harlan and Wesley. They had a baby sister younger than Wesley. Coming up, with so many mouths to feed and a pa who was too drunk to tend his fields, nothing resembling fondness had developed between the older and younger Mullen brothers, but Wesley was no more interested in farming than Harlan, and so he'd come to Denver with his older brother. In Denver, Harlan fell in with a conman who ran any number of schemes. Sometimes Wesley helped out – a fresh-faced boy always helped to build trust among the marks in a scam game. They did that for a couple of years before they fell in with Buddy Carver and Slap Duncan, and then they killed a man they were trying to steal from. It turned out the man they killed was the brother of a judge, and the entire world seemed to fall down around them. So they ran, first into the mountains, and then north.

"Think he's still coming after us?" Harlan asked.

Bearclaw Jim nodded his head.

"That man – whoever he is – ain't just out here in this valley knocking people over for fun," Bearclaw Jim said. "He's out here looking for somebody, and that somebody is probably us. I wouldn't be surprised if there ain't an entire posse with him. We need to keep moving and hope this snow don't let up."

Harlan Mullen understood the advantage of a heavy snow for covering tracks.

He glanced at the Indian woman. She'd not hardly said a word since they killed the old man back in town and brought her with them. He wasn't even certain she had much English, though she did seem to have some understanding of everything that was said to her or in front of her.

"Maybe we should leave her?" Mullen asked.

Bearclaw Jim shrugged his shoulders.

"She ain't none of my concern. Take her. Leave her. Shoot her and let the wolves have her, for all I care. But make your decision, because I'm riding on."

This was not Bearclaw Jim's outfit, and he was not interested in making their decisions.

Since losing his fingers, Bearclaw Jim had lost his ability to serve as a scout for the army. The army didn't want a one-handed guide who was useless in fight. He'd tried some, shooting with his bad hand, steadying a rifle steady with his left and pulling the trigger with the middle finger of his right hand. But the pain the vibrations sent through his stump was too much, and the rifle dang-near fell out of his weakened grip every time.

Without any way of making money, he'd gone through the winter, spring, and summer in town living on the little he had saved from the army.

But with winter coming on early this year, Bearclaw Jim found himself down to almost no money, and no prospects. He couldn't make it as a gambler – he'd lost half of what he had saved.

Then this outfit of young rascals came to him, talking about wanting to get someplace else in a hurry. He knew these boys. Most of the money he'd lost gambling had gone to them down at the saloon in town. He was all but certain they were cheating him, but he didn't know how they did it.

But they said they'd pay him, and pay him well, to get them out of town. They didn't care where, just somewhere far away.

Bearclaw Jim had it in his mind to take them up to Varina – what some folks were now calling Virginia City. He'd had a thought that if he couldn't scout for the army and couldn't grip a knife to clean a beaver pelt, well maybe he could hold a pan well enough to find some gold.

When Harlan Mullen first came to him about acting as a guide for the outfit, there was plenty of time to get north before bad weather. That was back a month or more ago.

But Mullen and his outfit kept pushing it off, delaying their departure. When they were finally ready to leave, they wanted to move out in a hurry. Bearclaw Jim figured they'd left someone dead in the town, but he didn't ask questions. None of that was his concern. Accepting guide wages, Bearclaw Jim could get back some of his losses from the gambling table, maybe enough to see him through a winter.

He also didn't ask about the woman. She was none of his concern.

He packed his mule and horse, forgot about the debts he owed around town, and within a couple of hours, the one-time army scout led the four men and the Indian woman out of town.

If they had to make a run from a posse, that didn't concern Bearclaw Jim none. He could lead 'em fast as easy as he could lead 'em slow. And if the posse caught up to them, Bearclaw Jim intended to slip off and get away. He wasn't going to fight it out.

But as he rode along, Bearclaw Jim thought about that man who stepped out of the darkness and so deftly put the younger Mullen boy on his backside. He could not say for sure, but old Bearclaw Jim couldn't help but think of the man who shot his hand away.

- 7 -

It took two days more of riding through the valley to reach the hills ahead of the western pass. Through that time, the snow continued to fall in bursts of not more than a couple of hours. But there were enough breaks in the snow that Moses Calhoun could follow the tracks of the men in front of him. The snow was thick enough that the tall meadow grass was all turned down, now, but the sagebrush standing up out of the snow dotted the white meadow with gray skeletal shapes reaching up from the ground.

A dense, gray fog hung thick over the valley,

shielding the mountains ahead.

After Calhoun left the party to pursue the men who had Aka Ne'ai, Sheriff Wooten and the man named Irwin decided they would both take Wesley Mullen back to the town. They put Mullen on a mule and turned over most of their provisions to Henry Chatham and Paul Bentsen who set out to catch up to Calhoun as fast as they could. They caught him about midday and then remained with him.

For two days they followed the valley west. Calhoun judged their progress from his knowledge of the valley, having hunted here for many years. The mountains ahead remained invisible for most of the time, hidden behind the thick fog, right up until they came to the place where the meadow began to roll in hills and valleys, the harsher terrain a signal that they were close to the slope of the mountain. There, the gray fog ahead of them seemed darker, and Calhoun knew the darkness was in fact the high mountain ahead.

And then up ahead a wall of pine and spruce seemed to rise up out of the fog, and Calhoun knew they had at last reached the mountain forest.

"It'll take all of today to reach the pass," Calhoun told Chatham. "We'll be going through the forest most of the way from here, and there will be places where we'll have to dismount to make the slope."

In the wall of trees ahead, Calhoun found what he was looking for – a wide path that would prove easy for the horse.

"It's a buffalo trail," Calhoun said. "If we see buffalo, and we probably will, give them a wide berth."

"Is this the trail Harlan Mullen and the others took?" Chatham asked.

"It is," Calhoun said.

"How can you be sure?"

Calhoun pointed to a small brown mound of what looked to be mud but was not.

"One of their horses left us a sign," Calhoun said.

For the past two days, Moses Calhoun was convinced the men he was chasing were not more than four hours ahead. They were moving fast, and if it was indeed Bearclaw Jim guiding their party, he so far had not made a mistake.

They started along the buffalo trail, following it maybe a couple of miles into the forest. After some time, Calhoun swung himself down out of his saddle and led his horse and mule off the natural trail.

"We're on foot for a while now," he said.

The men followed a ridge over a deep, wide draw. On the hill across from them on the other side of the draw, a large, round object appeared in the distance through the grayness ahead. As they neared it, Calhoun saw the big grizzly bear pick up its head and study them. After a moment, the bear decided they wouldn't be worth the effort, and he took off at a run back up the other side of the draw.

The canopy from the tall lodgepole pines and spruce provided a break from the snow, but it also meant the tracks on the ground were harder to follow. The snow here piled in patches between the trees, but in large swaths the ground was still bare. But Bearclaw Jim was following a predictable path, using the same switchbacks that Moses Calhoun had used on many hunts.

They moved up the slope, cutting between large

boulders and through the forest trees that whipped them as they passed. The entire time, they worked slowly to the north where they would find the saddle that provided a pass between the two large mountains.

"The saddle is a bare meadow," Calhoun warned them. "It's above the tree line, and the snow could be much worse there than it has been down below. We'll make it through, but it might not be easy going."

"We won't catch them up before they reach the pass?" Chatham asked, clearly disappointed.

"I don't see how we could."

Through the late afternoon the three men and their animals continued to work their way through the forest. On a ridge they stopped to rest for a little while. From the ridge, they had a muted view down into the long valley they had traveled for the past few days. The thick gray fog prevented them from picking out details, but it gave them the first opportunity to appreciate how high they had climbed.

They went on for another mile or so, and near the base of a tall rock face, Calhoun stopped again.

"We'll make camp here," he said. "Night will be on us soon, and I'd just as soon be warm and dry before it comes."

"I wish it wasn't so hard," Paul Bentsen said.

The boy was exhausted. The climb and the snow had taken everything out of him. His wool coat, fine for a man walking from his home to the store, was poor covering for this weather in these elements.

He sat back against a large boulder, but there was something clumsy about the way he did it so that he seemed almost to collapse on the thing. His eyes sagged and his chest rose and fell with heavy breaths.

"Nothing in these mountains is easy," Moses Calhoun said. "If the grizz or a mountain lion don't kill you, the snow or a high river will. Collect some firewood. Anything dry that you can find will serve. Let's see if we can keep from getting killed one more night."

Moses Calhoun's cautious nature usually prevented him from building up a large fire. There were those in the mountains who believed a fire would keep bear and cougar away, but Calhoun had seen it for himself that the predatory animals in the mountains associated a campfire with food and would come to scout. Lions seldom attacked a full-grown man, though they might, and a grizz would eat everything in the camp, including the man. So Calhoun was cautious about the size of the fire he built, he was careful about what food he cooked on it. Most often, he would cook a meal and then pack a mile or so away to make his camp.

But the thing that worried him most about a large fire was how it attracted the worst predator in the mountains – other men.

Whether it was Indians or trappers or men like the Mullen brothers and their outfit, Moses Calhoun knew that a large fire at camp could attract danger.

But Chatham and Bentsen insisted on a fire. Both men were cold to the bone, and wet, and so they ringed large rocks and built up a big fire that glowed in the small clearing where they'd erected one of the tents.

Seeing how they intended to camp, Calhoun went up the slope about twenty yards and scouted for a place where no animals had come through. He found a growth of low brush and used his knife to clear it out, and then he put down a bed of spruce branches before making a shelter. It was extra work, but Calhoun did not want to make a camp in a cleared space that might be part of a natural trail where bears or cougars might pass by.

After making his shelter, and still having a half hour of dusk to see by, Calhoun walked down to the roaring fire.

Both Chatham and Bentsen were sitting up near to their fire. The flames were high, and the coals put off a powerful warmth.

"Mind if I sit?" Calhoun asked.

Neither Chatham nor Bentsen were much surprised when the mountain man made his shelter at some distance from them. From the start, he'd separated himself from the other men. He rode ahead of them on the trail, camped at a distance, and sometimes went all day only sparing a few words for them.

"Sit, Calhoun," Henry Chatham said. "So you think we'll make the pass tomorrow?"

Calhoun slid off his boots and his socks, setting them on the rocks by the fire to try to dry them. He hated cold feet more than anything, and his wool socks were soddened and freezing.

"We should," Calhoun said, stretching his legs up near the fire to thaw out his feet.

"You think Mullen and them others have made the pass yet?" Chatham asked.

"I doubt it," Calhoun said. "We're still climbing, and moving around the edge of the base of the mountain. The last push up to the pass is a tough climb. I don't think they're so far ahead of us that they could make it today, and then they've got to be worried that they're above the tree line after dark – no fuel for a fire, no trees to make shelter. Just out there in the snow, trying to make their way across the pass and all exposed to the wind. They camped this side of the pass tonight."

Calhoun adjusted his boots and socks, trying to get them closer to the flames without singeing them.

The luxury of a fire reminded him of home. Kee Kuttai would be sending the boys to bed now. A couple of candles were probably lit, and the fire in the fireplace would be going pretty strong so that it would burn through most of the night.

In all the years they'd lived together in that cabin, and the years that Moses lived at the same home site before Kee Kuttai was there, he'd only seen a few black bear come near. Never a grizz, never any mountain lions. Sometimes buffalo wandered through the meadow beside the cabin. He'd never had trouble with hostile Indians there, nor had any troublemakers from the town come up. Calhoun's only concern in leaving his family was that if he did not come back. Kee Kuttai and the boys could make it through a winter alone if they had to, but they'd be hard pressed beyond that.

He wanted to get this over soon, and he had to keep reminding himself that his reason for being here was to try to save Aka Ne'ai, his old friend's daughter.

After a while, Calhoun checked his socks. They were warm, even if they weren't dry, so he slid them onto his feet. His boots were dry enough, and also warm.

He did not like to sit around camp without his footwear. Anything could happen, and if he had to flee from a bear, he didn't want to have to do it barefooted. So with his foot gear back on, he said a good night to

Chatham and Bentsen, and then he made his way in the growing darkness up to his shelter above them.

Their fire was still burning, and neither man seemed interested in leaving it.

In his shelter, Calhoun could hear the occasional crackle or pop from the flames as the sap-filled soft wood of the pines sizzled and spit.

Starting to doze, with a thought of waking later to keep a watch, Calhoun heard the sorrel horse outside do a sputter step. Immediately, eyes were open and senses alert. Something in the brush outside had spooked the sorrel.

The forest outside Calhoun's shelter appeared like a wall of blackness. Whatever moonlight existed overhead was entirely muted by the thick clouds overhead and the forest canopy, and the only light that showed came from the flicker of the campfire. The Tennessee rifle would prove useless against a threat. So Moses Calhoun gripped the beaded handle of his hatchet, a gift from a Snake chief. Over the years, he'd become deft at fighting with it, the one side carried a sharpened edge and the other a round ball of heavy iron that could crush a mountain lion's skull.

Calhoun slid himself out of his shelter. He ran his face right into the branch from a small spruce sapling right outside the shelter.

The horse was moving but hadn't neighed or snorted to give away his position. Calhoun fumbled in the dark until he caught the horse's lead rope with his shin. It was taut. The sorrel was anxious about something. Calhoun stepped over the rope and took a couple of steps toward the fire.

He could see the silhouettes of Chatham and Bentsen still sitting by their fire, appearing as a couple of shadows in the dim orange light.

And then he heard off some distance to his left a tremendous crash through branches – Calhoun started, swinging his body toward the noise, ready to face cat or bear, whichever, until he heard the grumblings of a human being.

"Conchuckled branches!" a man growled. "Can't see a danged thing in these woods."

***

Moses Calhoun recognized Chester Klemp's grumbling.

"Chester?" he called out.

"Who's that?" a suspicious voice called back.

"Moses Calhoun."

"Is that your fire I've been smelling?"

"A piece of it's mine," Calhoun said.

"Where in hell are you?"

"Off to your right, Chester," Calhoun said. "Are you hurt?"

"Just tripped over a danged spruce branch," Chester Klemp said, and there was a physical strain in his voice and Moses knew he was picking himself up off the ground. "About froze to the bone. Mind if I sit by your fire?"

"You're welcome," Calhoun said. "I'll meet you down

there."

Calhoun made his way slowly down to the fire.

Henry Chatham was standing now, one of his six-shooters clutched in his hand.

"Who's that out there?" Chatham asked.

"Put your gun away," Calhoun said. "He's a friend. Has a cabin not too far from here."

The thought of spending the night in Chester Klemp's cabin had crossed Calhoun's mind. Chester lived up on a ridge not far from the mountain pass, and Calhoun had found comfort in that cabin as a welcome visitor many times. But Calhoun also knew that Chester Klemp lived in these mountains to stay clear of a couple of warrants signed by judges with his name on them down below. Chester had gotten himself into trouble somewhere, maybe Missouri or Kansas or maybe both, and he'd fled a hanging rope into the mountains. He was a book reader, and his cabin was more fortified with books and candles than any Calhoun had ever seen before. But Chester was not a natural mountain man. He weathered his winters with difficulty and fared little better in the summers, and from one season to the next, Moses Calhoun always expected that someone would find Chester the victim of a fall or a bear.

The warrants, and his traveling companion being a man who earned his living on bounties, is what made Calhoun decide to avoid Chester's cabin.

"Who's that you've got with you?" a voice called from the blackness.

"A couple of bounty hunters," Calhoun said. "Looking for the men who killed Eli Simmons back in the town."

There was a long, silent pause.

"I didn't know Old Eli was killed," Chester said.

"Come on down and warm yourself by the fire," Calhoun said. "Nobody here means you no harm."

In a moment, Chester appeared in the firelight ringing the fire.

"Obliged to you, Mose," he said, stepping up to the fire. He slid off his gloves and held his hands out.

"Not the sort of night I'd expect to find you out and about," Calhoun said.

"It ain't by choice, I can tell you that," Chester said.

"How's that?" Calhoun asked, narrowing his eyes.

"I was out this afternoon, taking a walk down to the creek just to admire the snow, and when I come back, I see a passel of horses and a couple of men at my cabin."

"Is that right?" Calhoun said, taking a glance at Henry Chatham. Chatham's ears were perked.

"They busted right on in and made theirselves at home," Chester said. "I took it as a sign of trouble, and decided to bed down outside. I figured I could survive the snow for one night and hope they'd be gone in the morning."

"Think they just happened upon your place?" Calhoun asked.

"Must have," Chester said. "Visitors that come looking for me are a rare sight."

"You say there was two of them?" Chatham asked.

"Two outside," Chester said. "But there were others inside. I couldn't tell you how many."

Chatham turned to Moses Calhoun.

"That our men?"

Calhoun nodded.

"I would suspect so," he said. "I haven't seen any other tracks to suggest someone else is wandering around."

"They killed Old Eli, huh?" Chester asked.

The man was still not relaxed, though he stood close to the fire, and Calhoun watched as several times Chester gave a worried glance down at Henry Chatham. And Calhoun noticed, too, that Henry Chatham had caught one or two of those worried glances.

"Have seat," Chatham said. "Tell us about yourself."

Moses Calhoun cut him off.

"I reckon I wish you'd tell us more about these men up at your cabin," Calhoun said. "Did you see if they was armed?"

Chester sat on the bare ground by the fire and set his feet up near the ring of rocks so that he could warm his feet a touch.

"Oh, yes, Mose. They was heavily armed. Rifles and pistols, both."

Chester did not mention the knives on their belts, but it went without saying that a man carried a knife on his belt.

"Young men, both of them. Not boys, certainly, but younger than you or I, Mose."

"I've been tracking these men since Denver," Chatham interrupted. "If they're so close, I say we make our way up to this cabin tonight."

Moses Calhoun had already thought of trying to corner the men in the cabin and had dismissed it as a poor notion.

"It would be a poor plan to try to pin them in that cabin," Calhoun said. "Chester can correct me if I'm wrong, but I would guess they're provisioned enough in there to get through the entirety of the winter." Calhoun purposefully did not use Chester Klemp's full name.

"There ain't a lot of meat in the cabin. That's in my little smokehouse. But they'd sure get through a few weeks on flour and preserves I have stored away inside," Chester said.

Calhoun nodded.

"We wouldn't last more than a few days trying to wait them out," Calhoun said. "We'd be stuck out in the elements, the cold and the snow, and we'd be without provisions. But they could last weeks inside that cabin."

"Then we get them when they come out," Henry Chatham said.

"That would be my thinking," Calhoun agreed.

Moses Calhoun spent the next half-hour down by the light of the fire, cutting spruce and fir branches and weaving them into a shelter for Chester Klemp. Chester could get by okay hunting and reading his books so long as he was warm in his cabin, but anything beyond that – surviving a winter night outside of his cabin – became too much to ask. He was no woodsman, and Moses Calhoun figured that whatever trouble Chester got in down below must have been in a city somewhere.

When he was finished with the shelter, Calhoun went up to his own to sleep for a bit. But before he left, he laid out his intentions for Henry Chatham.

"Come first light, I'm going to make my way up to Chester's cabin, and I'm going to sit out there and wait for those men to leave. When they go, I'm going to get between them and the cabin so they've got no place to run back to, and I'm going to do what I have to do to set Aka Ne'ai free."

Henry Chatham nodded his head.

"That's okay by me, Mr. Calhoun," he said. "Like I told you before, I can get paid on those men whether I bring them back kicking and screaming or tied over the back of a mule. You want help, or are you intending to do this on your own?"

"Come or stay," Calhoun said. "But don't do anything that jeopardizes that Indian woman."

Chatham nodded.

Calhoun went off to his shelter, but Bentsen and Chatham both continued to sit by the fire.

"The easiest way of this is to shoot these men dead," Chatham told Bentsen. "If we try to take them out of these mountains as our prisoners, we'll be fighting them and watching them the entire way. So come morning, don't you hesitate to shoot if you've got the chance."

- 8 -

Bearclaw Jim took the bed, and no one argued with him about it.

He'd found over the years that except when he was scouting the army, he always could do what he wanted. Take an extra helping of supper. Take the best bed, or in this case the only bed. Take the first pick of whatever was being offered. People needed their guides to keep them alive, and so they never did argue when the guide was the first one in line for chow. Harlan Mullen and his crowd were no different. They stepped aside when Bearclaw Jim said he was sleeping in the bed.

He probably could have taken a piece of that Indian gal, if he wanted.

Harlan Mullen was keeping her pretty close, and so far, Bearclaw Jim had not seen Mullen make any hard use of her.

But Bearclaw Jim didn't want anything to do with her. This one had a mite too much spirit for his liking, and he worried she'd put up a fight. Some men preferred a gal with some spunk, but Jim liked them best when their spirits were broke. This one had hateful eyes, and the fact that she had her white father's blue eyes made it all the more worse. Still, spring was a long time off, and before long all the men in this cabin were going to want a piece of her.

"Any idea who this cabin belongs to?" Harlan Mullen asked.

Mullen was seated at the table. He'd found stew cooking in the pot on the fire, and had helped himself to it.

"Whoever it is knows we're here by now," Bearclaw Jim said. "He must've come home and seen us or seen the horses."

"What makes you say so?" Mullen asked.

"On account of it being full on dark outside now," Jim said. "Man had stew simmering in the pot. That was his supper tonight. He intended to be home by dark."

Mullen frowned at the stew. He didn't like the idea that there was someone outside who knew where they were.

"We could stay here for the winter," he said.

"We could, at that," Bearclaw Jim said. "I didn't look

inside his smokehouse, but I reckon it's going to be slap full of meat, all stored up for the winter."

Bearclaw Jim's impression of Harlan Mullen rose quite a bit when the man had the good sense to abandon his brother. A weaker, more foolish man would have insisted on riding after his brother and trying to save him. But Harlan Mullen was a survivor, and Bearclaw Jim preferred to associate himself with survivors.

The other two men were hangers-on of the worst sort.

Slap Duncan and Buddy Carver, between them, had never had an original thought. They followed along behind Harlan Mullen because Harlan kept them alive. It amused Bearclaw Jim that neither of them had come to realize that if Harlan Mullen would turn his back on his own brother, he'd just as quick turn his back on the two of them.

Buddy Carver was particularly loathsome to Bearclaw Jim because Buddy Carver was a moaner. He complained non-stop about the cold and the snow and the state of his frozen toes and his frozen nose and his frozen ass. At least Slap Duncan kept his mouth shut most of the time.

"It'll be tight quarters for five or six months," Buddy Carver said. With much complaint, he'd piled a couple of blankets in a spot not far from the fireplace and was now reclined there with his boots and socks off and his feet pointed toward the fire.

"It would be at that," Harlan Mullen said. "But it's better than getting caught by a blizzard between here and them goldfields."

Harlan took a few bites of the stew.

"What do you think, old timer?" he said to Bearclaw Jim. "You know these mountains better than me and the boys. Are we better off to hole-up here, or should we press on?"

Bearclaw Jim swung his head from side-to-side trying to make up his mind.

"It could clear," he said. "First snow of the year doesn't always last. In the next couple of days if it warms some and the snow melts, we could probably make Virginia City without too much trouble. But you boys waited too long to get started."

Harlan walked over to the Indian woman who was sitting on a woven blanket. He took her roughly by the wrist and pulled her to a standing position. Then he wrapped a rope around her wrists and tied it tight so that her hands were bound. He tied the loose end to his own ankle. This was how he'd done it every night since they set out so as to keep her from trying to sneak off.

"Well then, we'll wait it out here," Harlan said. "If that means waiting it out for a couple of days, that's fine. If it means waiting it out for five or six months, we can do that, too."

- 9 -

Chester Klemp watched his breath form a fog in front of his face.

His fingers and toes stung they were so cold. Overnight the clouds had disappeared, and the morning sun came through the pines with renewed intensity, gleaming off the snow and blinding even in the shadows of the forest. Moses Calhoun was a little ways in front of Chester Klemp, hunkered down in a squat behind a fir tree. Motionless under his heavy bearskin coat, Moses looked less like a man and more like a large predator. The coat, of course, made him seem bearlike, but the way he was hunched down in a squat, he looked like a big cat ready to pounce. A mountain lion with the size and strength of a bear.

Tekaiten Toi-yah'-to'-ko – Cougar Killer.

That's what the Snake People called him, and it was a name Moses Calhoun had earned many years ago when he saved the young son of a Snake chief. Chester heard the story from others who knew it. Moses Calhoun never spoke of it unless asked, and even then dismissed it as a small thing that had happened once. He was not a boastful man.

Chester picked his steps out carefully, avoiding patches of snow where his feet might crunch and make unnecessary noise, though they were far enough from the cabin that he did not think anyone would hear crunching snow.

He stepped close behind Calhoun and then squatted down in a similar fashion. Then Chester whispered at the back of Calhoun's head.

"Those men killed Old Eli Simmons?" he said.

"That's what them others told me," Moses said. "And it's Eli's daughter they have."

Chester nodded thoughtfully. In a place where men came for solitude and to be away from other men, friendships did not come easily. Most of the men who called these mountains home had a distrust of other men. Their friends, often as not, were horses or mules, or dogs, maybe. Some of them stayed so long and lonesome in the mountains that they started having conversations with their traps or the beaver they clubbed to death and skinned. True friendship, like a precious metal, proved a rarity for most.

"I reckon I don't blame you much for wanting to kill those men," Chester Klemp said. "Them killing your friend. But I'd be obliged if you would make certain sure them fellers with you don't shoot hell out of my cabin. The little I have in there is all I have."

Calhoun made a dismissive noise.

"I don't want to kill those men," he said.

Chester frowned at the back of Calhoun's head.

"How's that?"

"I just want to get the woman back unhurt," Calhoun said.

Chester chewed his lip for a moment and then wished he hadn't. As soon as his teeth turned loose of the lip, it liked to froze in the cold air.

"They killed your friend," Chester said. "You mean to say you didn't ride up here to pay them back for that?"

Moses Calhoun stayed quiet for several long moments. He sniffed a bit and then blew out a puff of breath that turned to fog in front of his face.

"Revenge is a bad game," Calhoun said. "You can't win at something like that. You hate a man enough to seek revenge against him, and that hate will eat you up until you're no better than the thing you hate. If I have to kill those men to save Eli's daughter, I'll do it. But that's not why I'm here."

Chester frowned again. In his own life, revenge seemed the natural course of things, though it had proved a losing game. The warrants against Chester Klemp down below accused him of murder, which was true enough. But he always thought of it less as murder and more as collecting a debt. He killed a couple of men who owed him for a killing they'd done. Two men in Independence, Missouri, shot and killed his brother in a robbery. A jury saw it different. Said those men were defending their own lives. But the fact was, the men killed Chester's brother to steal from him. So Chester took it upon himself to collect what they owed. A life for a life.

But maybe Moses Calhoun had a point. Here he was, Chester, living in the remote mountains where he didn't have a friend, didn't have much of a life, and all to avoid warrants he earned from paying back the trespasses against him. Maybe in taking his revenge, he had ended up the worse for it.

"You sweet on Eli's daughter?" Chester whispered. "I thought you had a squaw."

"I'm married," Moses said, allowing a bit of annoyance to slip into his tone. He knew how some men felt about their "squaws" and it perturbed him to hear Chester call Kee Kuttai by the name. "I don't want Eli's daughter for myself. The way I see it, if something happened to me, and my wife was taken by men like these, I would hope that someone would come and rescue her. So I'm doing for my friend what I hope some friend would do for me."

Chester nodded. It was an answer he could accept.

"How come they ain't come out yet?" he asked.

"Judging by the smoke coming from your chimney, they're enjoying theirselves some warmth," Moses Calhoun said.

The two men continued to sit in silence, watching the smoke rise from the cabin's chimney, hidden in their cold perches from behind the branches of the fir tree.

The horses in Chester's paddock picked grass through the snow and ate at his store of hay. Birds sang songs through the forest. Snow let loose from high up branches and crashed down to the ground below. The sun moved through the branches above. But no one inside the cabin seemed eager to make a move outside, and the men in there also did not appear intent on making tracks for the Valley of Flowers, or anywhere else.

Commotion and cursing within the branches of a fir tree behind them announced Henry Chatham's arrival.

Seeing the two men squatting behind the fir tree, Chatham adopted a similar position.

"You're supposed to be with the horses," Moses Calhoun said to him.

"I left Bentsen with the horses," Chatham said. "So what's going on in there?"

"They're in there," Calhoun said. "But they've not shown themselves yet."

"Then maybe we should go in after them," Henry Chatham suggested. "It's better than freezing out here waiting."

Calhoun did not answer the man with anything more than a shrug of his shoulders, and even then, the shrug was almost imperceptible under his big coat.

In the continuing silence, Henry Chatham got increasingly frustrated.

"Maybe I need to take charge here," Chatham said.

"I'm not going to do anything – or allow anything to be done – that's going to put that woman in jeopardy," Moses Calhoun said. "We'll have an opportunity, and we just need to be ready when it comes along."

Even as he said it, the three men saw the door of the cabin crack open, and a figure appeared in the doorway. In a moment, a man stepped out onto Chester Klemp's porch, his boots heavy on the wooden slats of the porch. He pulled the door shut and then stepped around to the side of the porch, looking back behind the cabin where the small smokehouse was located.

"That's Buddy Carver," Chatham whispered.

- 10 -

Chester Klemp was smart about his smokehouse. A man had to be. Grizzlies would tear through it if it was not constructed with the specific purpose of keeping them out. Even then, a man might expect to lose some portion of his winter store.

Chester located the smokehouse a safe distance away from his cabin, but within rifle shot. He'd erected a snake fence around it – nothing that would keep a grizzly out, but something that would cause a loud disturbance as the grizzly made his way through the fence. It was Chester's expectation that such a disturbance would give him an opportunity to make a rifle shot at the bear before it consumed all his meat.

Chester made the smokehouse's foundation from large rocks mortared together with a mixture of clay and river sand and ash – the same chinking mixture he used to mortar the walls of his cabin. He finished it off in the style of a log cabin, taking more care than he did even with his own cabin.

But the distance from cabin to smokehouse is what convinced Moses Calhoun that he had an opportunity.

As Buddy Carver walked toward the smokehouse, his back to the trees where Calhoun and the others remained hidden, Moses Calhoun slid out of his heavy bearskin coat, gripped the head of his hatchet, and stepped out from behind the fir trees that had hidden him from view.

Calhoun made no noise, stepping softly through the pine straw and avoiding patches of snow. He glanced back and forth between Carver and the cabin to be certain no one inside the cabin came out and caught him hanging in the wind. He moved quickly toward Carver, who meandered unconcerned toward the smokehouse. As he passed by the cabin, Calhoun could hear voices inside.

At the snake fence, Carver stopped to slide away the top split rail on one section of fence so that he could access the smokehouse. He stepped over the other rails, and in that moment that he stood straddling the fence, the man known among the Snake people as Tekaiten Toi-yah'-to'-ko pounced like a big cat.

Calhoun sprang forward, covering the last few yards in three or four big leaps, and as he jumped out at Carver, he also swung the heavy, blunt end of the hatchet's head.

The two men went down in a heap between the snake fence and the smokehouse.

Calhoun's leather-gloved fist, still gripping the hatchet, pounded twice, and a third time, into Carver's face.

The man had shouted in surprise, but the noise was clipped short when Calhoun knocked the breath out of him. Now, his face bloodied from the three hard punches, Carver found himself too dazed to fight back or holler for help.

"If you make a sound, I'll bury this hatchet in your throat," Calhoun vowed.

Buddy Carver, shocked and battered by the sudden attack, gave a feeble, submissive nod of his head.

Already Calhoun had found the six-shooter on the man's hip and slid it from its holster, tossing it aside in the snow near the smokehouse.

"We're going to walk back into those trees over yonder," Calhoun said with a nod of his head toward the trees behind them. "You're going to go out front of me, and you're going to be quiet about it. If you make a sound, I'm going to bury this hatchet in your back so hard that you see it one more time before you die. You think you can manage to keep your mouth shut?"

Again, Carver gave a submissive nod. Blood from his nose covered his eyes so thick he could hardly see, but he stank of fear.

Calhoun got to his feet and pulled Carver up from the ground. Leading the man with a hand in his back and his other hand gripping the hatchet, Calhoun pushed Carver toward the cover of trees and then walked him back to where Chatham and Chester Klemp were waiting.

"That was a fine piece of work, but there's still three men inside the cabin," Chatham said.

Calhoun ignored the bounty hunter.

"What are their intentions inside?" Calhoun asked.

Carver shook his head, refusing to answer, but Henry Chatham gave him a sharp crack on the back of the head with the handle on his six-shooter.

"Answer the question, Carver," Chatham said.

Carver winced and furrowed his brow, but that just brought back the pain from the bridge of his nose. He coughed and spit blood into the snow.

"They's studying on staying a few days," Carver said.

"Is the woman still in there?" Calhoun asked.

"That squaw?" Carver said.

"Is she still in there?" Calhoun asked.

"She's in there."

"And Bearclaw Jim?" Calhoun asked.

"He's in there," Carver confirmed.

"Harlan, Slap Duncan, this Bearclaw feller," Chatham said. "And the squaw. Anyone else?"

"That's all they is," Carver said.

Calhoun glanced over at Chester Klemp.

"Take him back to Bentsen and the horses," Calhoun said. "Bind his wrists behind good."

Chester nodded and took Buddy Carver by the shoulders, leading him back through the woods to where Paul Bentsen waited with the horses.

"Now what?" Chatham said.

Though Henry Chatham considered himself to be in charge now that Sheriff Wooten was gone, he had so far acquiesced to the man who called these mountains home. Chatham found that it was prudent to let Calhoun dictate the terms of their pursuit. He suspected that at some point they would come to a parting of ways, but for now Moses Calhoun was proving useful to him.

"We'll not do anything that endangers the woman inside," Calhoun said.

"Ain't you already done that by jumping Buddy Carver?" Chatham asked.

Calhoun nodded slightly.

"Maybe," he said. "I'm hoping one or two of those still inside might come out looking for him. If that happens, we've got a chance to quickly diminish their numbers. Bearclaw Jim worries me, though. He's an old army scout, and he had a knack for surviving."

Chatham shook his head.

"I don't have no warrant for him. He ain't my concern unless he tries to stop me from bringing in the other two."

"Warrants ain't my concern," Calhoun said. "The woman is all I'm here for."

The two men were standing in conversation and being less careful than they might have been, so when Harlan Mullen cracked open the door of the cabin and looked around, neither Calhoun nor Chatham noticed. It was not until they heard Mullen's boots on the plank boards of the front porch that both men grew silent and squatted back down behind the fir.

"That's Harlan Mullen," Chatham said, pushing a fir branch down with the barrel of his six-shooter.

Both Calhoun and Chatham squatted lower, watching Mullen as he stepped around to the side of the cabin's porch and looked back toward the smokehouse.

"Buddy?" Harlan called at the smokehouse.

"We can't get to him before he could get back to the cabin door," Calhoun whispered.

"But we can block him from getting back to the cabin door," Chatham said, and the man sprang to his feet, pushed through the branches of the fir tree and leveled his revolver.

Harlan Mullen heard the commotion and turned on his heel. Seeing Chatham, he started back toward the cabin. Chatham took a shot with his six-gun, the explosion from the gun shaking awake the quiet of the forest.

Mullen danced backwards. The bullet embedded in the soft spruce log of the cabin wall dangerously close to where Harlan Mullen was standing.

Already Chatham was drawing his second gun and cocking back the hammer on the first. He let loose with a two-gun volley, and while his shot sprang wide of Mullen, it was clear to Mullen and Calhoun both that Henry Chatham was shooting to kill.

The shots were striking the wall between Mullen and the cabin door, so Mullen spun on his heel again and charged back toward the smokehouse.

Chatham fired another volley as Mullen attempted to clear the snake fence, and Calhoun saw Mullen rise up and then fall into the snow in the clearing between the fence and the smokehouse. He was in almost the same place where Calhoun had knocked Buddy Carver to the ground.

Wounded, Harlan Mullen scrambled to his feet. That's when he spotted Carver's six-shooter on the ground near the edge of the cabin. He dove for it, sprawling on the ground. He then rolled and stumbled to his feet, making for the door of the smokehouse.

Chatham drew back the hammers on both guns, and then took special care as he aimed down the barrel of his right-hand gun.

Mullen snatched open the door of the smokehouse and rushed headlong inside just as Chatham got off another shot.

Mullen let loose an expletive, and Calhoun couldn't tell if the man was now shot twice or just cussing at his bad luck.

***

"Come on out, Harlan!" Henry Chatham shouted. "You don't stand a lick of a chance in there. We've got the cabin and the smokehouse surrounded."

From inside the smokehouse they could hear cursing. Harlan Mullen had been hit at least once, maybe twice, and the blood in the snow where he had fallen suggested he might have taken on a pretty bad wound.

"What's going on out there?" a timid voice called from inside the cabin.

"Slap Duncan, you throw your gun out the door and then follow it out with your hands reaching for heaven,"

Henry Chatham said.

"Don't you do it, Slap!" Harlan Mullen shouted from inside the smokehouse, and Henry Chatham responded by firing an unnecessary bullet into the side of the smokehouse. "You stay in that cabin and shoot any man that tries to come in."

Moses Calhoun still watched from behind the fir tree, but now he picked up his old Tennessee rifle and stepped past the branches of the fir up to where Henry Chatham was squared off with a gun in each hand.

"I reckon Chester built that smokehouse to keep bears out," he said. "I doubt that little gun is powerful enough to knock it down."

Chatham ignored him.

"What do you plan to do now?" Calhoun asked.

"Wait for them to surrender," Chatham said. "You keep a gun on that smokehouse, and if Harlan Mullen shows his head, you shoot that sucker right off."

Calhoun chewed his lip for a moment.

"That woman in the cabin," he said. "You've come out and exposed us, and maybe put her life in jeopardy. If anything happens to her, I'll hold you to account."

Chatham worked his way a bit closer to the cabin and then hunkered down behind a large boulder. Calhoun put a thick-trunked lodgepole pine between him and the smokehouse and then leaned against it, keeping one eye on the smokehouse and the other on Henry Chatham. He was opposed to this plan, that seemed to lack any planning, and he was angry that Chatham had moved out on his own. Not that he'd done anything different when he jumped Buddy Carver, but at least he managed to do it without alerting the men inside the cabin.

"Come on out of there, Slap," Chatham called at the cabin. "We've got you separated and surrounded, now. Throw out that gun and give yourself up."

"How do you know my name?" Slap Duncan shouted from inside the cabin. There was panic in the man's voice, and Calhoun studied Chatham for a moment. Though he did not seem to know these men personally, he did seem to understand them. He'd identified Slap Duncan as a weaker man, and now that he was outside of Harlan Mullen's influence, Chatham was working on Duncan, playing on those fears and insecurities. It might be a plan that would work. Though Calhoun wondered what influence Bearclaw Jim might wield on Slap Duncan inside the cabin.

"Don't you give up, Slap!" Harlan Mullen shouted from the smokehouse.

"Don't pay no attention to him, Slap," Chatham shouted at the cabin. "Mullen's shot. He ain't gonna live through the day."

There was silence for a moment, and then Slap Duncan called out.

"Harlan! Is you shot?"

"I'm all right," Harlan shouted. "Didn't do nothing but wing me."

"That sounds to me like a man in pain," Chatham said. "How bad are you bleeding, Harlan?"

Harlan stayed quiet, but from his position behind the lodgepole pine, Moses Calhoun could see the shutter over the window on the side of the cabin push open just a hair, and then it pushed open a bit wider. Calhoun didn't move. The person peering out hadn't noticed him as he was looking toward the front of the cabin, likely to see if he could get a shot at Henry Chatham.

The window pushed open a hair more.

Calhoun studied the distance and the crack in the shutter, wondering if he could get off a shot that would tell.

He could see enough of the man's face now to know it was Slap Duncan taking a look. Though it had been a year since he'd last seen Bearclaw Jim, Moses Calhoun knew he would recognize the man. This one, though he could only see a piece of his face, was much too young and thin to be the old army scout Bearclaw Jim.

"Give it up now, Slap," Chatham called out again. "You don't want to make us come in there and fetch you. That won't go well for you."

The head at the window disappeared back inside the cabin, but the shutter stayed open still.

"They's two of us in here, and we're both ready to make a stand," Slap Duncan said.

Chatham glanced over at Moses Calhoun, and Calhoun gave him a doubtful look and shook his head.

"Bearclaw Jim ain't making a stand," Henry Chatham shouted. "This ain't his fight, and he knows it. I've got warrants for you, Slap. Warrants for Harlan Mullen and his brother. Warrants for Buddy Carver. But that man in there, so long as he doesn't further involve himself, he's got nothing to fear from the law."

This was for Bearclaw Jim's benefit as much as it was for Slap Duncan. Henry Chatham was trying to even out the odds a little, get Jim to back out of this thing.

"In fact, if Bearclaw Jim was so inclined, I reckon he could open up the door of that cabin and walk right on past us and all our guns."

Moses Calhoun expected it would work. He knew enough about Bearclaw Jim to know that the man wasn't going to make a fight for Slap Duncan and Harlan Mullen. Jim was a man who looked out for himself. Calhoun also knew that Bearclaw Jim wasn't likely to put up much of a fight, anyway. Calhoun had shot away half of the man's gun hand. He couldn't draw back a hammer or squeeze a trigger. The one problem might be if Bearclaw Jim figured that Moses Calhoun was outside. It seemed likely he'd be looking for revenge sooner or later.

"Don't you listen to him, Jim!" Harlan Mullen shouted. "We're all in this together."

But Harlan Mullen's imploring proved fruitless.

Inside the cabin there were heated voices, and then a shout. And then the door swung open wide.

Bearclaw Jim emerged, looking directly at Henry Chatham. Over his shoulder he had a possibles bag and a canteen. He carried a six-shooter on his belt, but even Bearclaw Jim would admit he was next to useless trying to shoot the thing with his left hand.

He kicked the door closed behind him.

"I've a horse and a pack mule," Jim said. "I expect to be allowed to gather them up."

"Do as you like," Chatham said. "Just don't stand between me and that cabin."

Jim nodded.

"Fair enough," he said.

His eyes scanned the trees around the cabin. His gaze fell on Moses Calhoun.

"I might have known you'd be riding with these men," Bearclaw Jim said. "You've got me at a disadvantage at the moment, Mr. Calhoun, but one day we'll meet on even terms."

Calhoun grinned and nodded. He did not speak, but he stretched his fist out toward Bearclaw Jim, and with a chuckle he raised his thumb up to the sky.

Jim spat at the ground, and then he heaved his saddle up over his shoulder with one hand and started toward the paddock where the men had turned out their horses.

"Good luck to you Harlan, and you, too, Slap," Bearclaw Jim called as he saddled his horse. "No hard feelings. If you make it out of this alive, I'll greet you as friends in the future."

"You ain't leaving!" Harlan Mullen shouted.

"I reckon that's the same thing your little brother said, Harlan," Henry Chatham shouted at the smokehouse. "But you sure did leave him. That was his brother, Slap. You think if Harlan sees a chance to make a run he'll leave you the way he left his brother?"

Moses Calhoun had given up watching the smokehouse very closely. Harlan Mullen wasn't coming out of there without Calhoun seeing it out of the corner of his eye. Instead, Calhoun's attention was on the paddock where Bearclaw Jim took his time to get the horse saddled. Bearclaw Jim was just the sort of man to make a treaty and then put a bullet in a man's back, and Calhoun wasn't going to give him the chance.

After some time, though, Jim got the horse saddled,

and he climbed up into the saddle and started to ride away, the horse going at a slow walk.

- 11 -

Several minutes after Bearclaw Jim rode out, Paul Bentsen came up through the trees behind Henry Chatham.

"Someone just rode past us on the trail south," Bentsen told Chatham.

Since Bearclaw Jim abandoned the others, Henry Chatham had continued his shouted taunts at Slap Duncan, all intended to weaken Duncan's resolve and convince him to give up.

"That's the guide who was leading them," Chatham

said. "It's all right. We let him go."

Chatham checked his guns. He'd fired several shots at Mullen, and with Bentsen now there he wanted to reload his empty chambers.

"You keep your rifle on that cabin," Chatham said. "If Slap Duncan shows his face, you shoot it off."

Bentsen raised up his rifle, checking to make sure he had a cap in place. Henry Chatham hurried to reload his six-shooters. Reloading the empty chambers was time consuming, and with his hands numb from the cold, the job was doubly difficult. He spilled powder in the snow and dropped several caps. At length, though, he managed to get the gun reloaded.

"Slap Duncan!" Chatham shouted. "I ain't gonna wait all day for you. You come on out and give yourself up, or I'm coming in there for you."

For some time there had been no sound from the smokehouse. Chatham hoped that Harlan Mullen was in the smokehouse dying. Harlan Mullen was a hard man and wouldn't be easily taken back to Colorado. Not that Chatham intended to get so far with him. He might take Carver or Duncan as a prisoner, and probably Wesley Mullen, too, but Chatham had already decided that Harlan Mullen wasn't coming off this mountain alive.

"Go and tell Calhoun to be ready," Chatham said to Bentsen. "Tell him to keep a watch on that smokehouse. You and me are going to bust open that cabin."

Bentsen swallowed hard. A young man yearns for adventure, but when it finds him, he often discovers he did not want it.

"We're just going to run in there?"

"Hell, yes," Chatham said. "I'm freezing out here, and I don't want this to run on into night."

Bentsen nodded.

In a crouch, he ran across the front of the cabin to the tree where Moses Calhoun was watching.

"Mr. Chatham says we're going to go into the cabin," Bentsen said. "He wants you to keep a watch on the smokehouse."

Calhoun shook his head.

"We're not doing anything to endanger that woman inside," he said. "You tell Chatham if he starts for that smokehouse, I'll shoot him dead before he gets there."

Paul Bentsen took a breath and then shook his head.

"I ain't gonna tell Mr. Chatham that."

Calhoun sighed heavily in frustration.

They were in a good position. Their quarry were separated, diminished, and surely dispirited. And one of them was hurt, maybe hurt seriously. The fact was, Chatham through luck or ingenuity had managed the affair pretty well so far. And neither Slap Duncan nor Harlan Mullen had yet to consider their one ace-in-the-hole. They had a prisoner, and threatening her life might buy them some advantage. But Old Eli's daughter, Aka Ne'ai, was a squaw, and these men hadn't considered that her life might hold some value as a bargaining chip.

Maybe a rush into the cabin was the thing.

Calhoun intended to go and talk it over with Chatham himself, leave Bentsen to keep an eye on the smokehouse. But just then Harlan Mullen started to make noise again.

"Hey, Slap!" he shouted from inside the smokehouse. "You remember when the posse came for us in that cabin outside of Denver?"

"I remember," Slap Duncan called back.

"You remember how we got loose?"

"I remember," Slap said.

There was a moment's pause. Then: "Let's do it that way again."

"I'm game," Slap Duncan said.

Calhoun glanced at Chatham who now had both his six-shooters drawn and was cocking back the hammer.

"Bentsen!" Chatham shouted. "Get back here."

Paul Bentsen shrugged at Calhoun and started to make a crouched run back toward Chatham, and that's when the cabin door flew open, banging loudly against the door frame. Slap Duncan stood there with a shotgun in one hand, held fast against his side with his elbow, and a six-shooter in the other hand. The shotgun he'd gotten down from above Chester Klemp's fireplace. The shotgun was Chester's emergency gun, packed with powder and shot enough to scare a bear or cut an intruder in half.

Paul Bentsen saw the armed man standing in the doorway and stopped his run, standing and looking.

The shotgun exploded.

Slap Duncan was aiming from the hip and didn't much care if he hit anything or not. The shotgun was for effect. He wanted to scare the men pinning him down, get them to duck their heads. The plan, as he understood it, was to get out of the cabin and in a position where he and Harlan could fight this thing out without being trapped.

But the shotgun's effect was more than Slap Duncan intended. He never even saw Paul Bentsen. Slap was looking down the barrel of the six-shooter at the boulder where Henry Chatham was hunkered.

Paul Bentsen caught the spread of the shotgun blast in his face and torso. Buckshot ripped through his chest and throat and face so that he twisted and fell, dying in the snow.

Slap worked the hammer on the six-shooter with his thumb, skipping .44-caliber balls across the top of the boulder.

Moses Calhoun brought the big Poor-Boy rifle up to his shoulder and squeezed the trigger. The heavy ball smashed into Slap Duncan at his armpit, leaving terrible damage through his upper torso.

Slap still had two full chambers in the six-shooter when he fell back against the wall of Chester Klemp's cabin.

Quickly, Moses Calhoun poured powder into the barrel of the Tennessee rifle. He used the ramrod to push the ball home. It was practiced effort. A man had to be fast at reloading his rifle. An elk might get away if he took too long. A wounded bear might get at him.

As he reloaded the rifle, he anticipated Harlan Mullen bursting out of the smokehouse the same way Slap Duncan came out of the cabin. At the first sound, Calhoun was ready to duck back behind his tree and drop to the ground.

But the door to the smokehouse never opened.

Aka Ne'ai appeared at the cabin door.

"Get back in there until it's safe!" Calhoun shouted at

her, and Eli Simmons' daughter didn't have to be told twice. She even pulled the door closed behind her.

Now Henry Chatham was bent over Slap Duncan. He kicked the six-shooter away, but the effort was unnecessary. Slap Duncan was dead on the ground. The hunter knew how to bring down his prey with a fatal shot.

Calhoun brought the rifle up to his shoulder and aimed it at the smokehouse, but the door remained fast.

Chatham moved from Slap Duncan to Paul Bentsen, and he rolled the young man onto his back. Bentsen was still alive, but not by much. His eyes were open and he seemed aware, but the shot had torn through his throat and he could not speak. The boy looked scared.

Chatham stood up and looked toward the smokehouse. He had both his six-shooters in his hands.

"You shot hell out of Slap Duncan," he told Calhoun. "Paul's alive, but ain't nothing we can do to save him now."

Moses Calhoun did not spare a glance to either the dead or the dying. Instead, he kept his eyes down the barrel of the Poor-Boy rifle, aiming at the door to the smokehouse, and aiming low in case Harlan threw open the door and appeared in a squat.

But the door did not open.

"Come on out of there," Henry Chatham shouted. "Slap's dead and it's just you, now, Harlan."

Chatham waited for a response, but none came.

Henry Chatham moved over to the corner of the cabin where he'd have some shelter.

"We can wait as long as you can," Chatham said.

"Might as well get this over with."

Still, Harlan Mullen did not respond.

After several minutes, Moses Calhoun lowered his rifle.

"He's gone," Calhoun said.

"What do you mean he's gone?"

"I mean he ain't in there," Calhoun said. "Man slipped out the back. He convinced Duncan to jump out of the cabin to give him cover, and he slipped out."

Chatham looked at the smokehouse and then back to Calhoun.

"What kind of smokehouse has a back door?" he asked.

"It doesn't," Calhoun said. "But it has a dirt floor. He's dug under it enough to slip out."

Chatham narrowed his eyes.

"How sure are you?"

"Sure enough," Calhoun said, and to prove it, he walked toward the smokehouse. He stepped over the snake fence and pulled on the door, but it was bound fast from the inside. Then Calhoun walked around to the back, and there he found a small hole dug out, just big enough for a narrow man to slip under the rock foundation of the cabin.

Moses Calhoun surveyed the woods behind the smokehouse, but he did not immediately see any sign of Harlan Mullen. What he did see, though, were splotches of red in the snow on the top rail of the snake fence.

Henry Chatham came around the side of the smokehouse and examined the hole at the foundation of the cabin.

"Dug his way out," he observed. "What now?"

Calhoun was still looking out through the forest. His eyes fell on a red patch of snow.

"I can track him," Calhoun said. "Go and fetch Chester and the prisoner. Gather up the horses. Go inside the cabin and see to that woman, make certain she's okay. Help Chester figure out how to pry open the door to his smokehouse. I figure Mullen must've tied it shut from the inside, so maybe you can wedge a knife in there to cut, or maybe someone will have to go through Harlan's hole. Y'all get yourselves warm. I'll be back with Harlan Mullen before dark."

- 12 -

Harlan Mullen cut a trail in a hurry.

As Calhoun started up the slope, following the traces of blood in the snow the same as he would if he was tracking an elk or a deer, he was surprised to find how deep into the woods Mullen had managed to get.

Tracking a man presented far more dangers than tracking a wounded animal. Calhoun knew that Harlan Mullen might have burrowed in somewhere and could be waiting for him, and Mullen would surely see Calhoun coming before Calhoun saw Mullen hunkered down and hiding. On the other hand, it was just as likely that Mullen kept moving, hoping to put as much distance as possible between himself and the men pursuing him.

The blood trail was not difficult to follow. The blood shone like a beacon in the snow, and Calhoun had to wonder if Mullen's wound would not soon get to him. Whatever he'd done in the smokehouse, he'd not successfully bandaged his wound yet.

The footprints in the snow, in those places where the snow was thick enough to follow footprints, showed Mullen's feet staying close together. This was not a man in a full run. Mullen was hurt, and he was limping. Likely the wound was on his right leg. The blood drops consistently fell beside the right footprints in the snow.

Still, the man had managed to move quickly and covered a lot of ground.

He'd followed a natural path through the forest behind Chester Klemp's cabin, a long draw rising at an easy slope. Whether by chance or intention, Harlan Mullen was making for the open pass. It would be covered in snow now, but still possible to get through without much difficulty. But more importantly, he was moving to where he would be out in the open, exposed with no good place to hide. That was where Calhoun wanted to find him. Here in the forest, with rocks and gullies and trees for cover, Mullen could hunker down and hide, wait for Calhoun, and shoot him down without warning.

So Moses Calhoun took his time. He never moved more than a few yards without pausing to scan the forest in front of him. Where possible, he used the trees to give himself shelter, examining the forest and following the trail of blood and footprints from a distance rather than carelessly following right along in the same path.

After several minutes, Calhoun realized he could no longer smell the chimney smoke from Chester Klemp's cabin. He figured he must have walked close to a mile now.

It was an unsettling thing to be deep in a forest on the side of a mountain, alone, and knowing there was another man not far away who was looking to kill you.

Moses Calhoun knew the feeling. He'd experienced troubles in these mountains before. Though he'd tried always to stay on friendly terms with the local Indians, a man never knew when he might encounter a rogue band determined to take out frustration or anger on the first white man they saw. The mountain hunter, though, could moderate the fear. He'd been stalked by mountain lion and bear, Indians and white soldiers. A wounded man, lost and alone, presented a different sort of foe, one that Calhoun should be cautious over, but not afraid. And so he settled his breathing, he kept his emotions in check, and he continued his pursuit.

But Calhoun knew that Harlan Mullen's mind must be spinning with the possibilities for a terrible end. Mullen was now like a wounded animal – confused, injured, afraid. Harlan Mullen, no matter how tough a man he might be, or how willing he was to abandon his friends and even his own brother, at this moment had to be pondering his own mortality. He was sure to make a mistake.

The shot came from a cluster of large rocks up on a ridge about fifty yards ahead of him.

Calhoun heard the boom of the gun and dropped down behind a pine trunk. The bullet whipped harmlessly through the branches of fir and spruce trees.

It would take a better gunman than Harlan Mullen to hit a target at fifty yards with a six-shooter.

From behind the trunk of the pine tree, Calhoun sought and found the white cloud of smoke that showed Mullen's location.

He searched down the barrel of his Tennessee rifle, but saw no human flesh to shoot at on the other side of the rocks. Fifty yards with the Poor-Boy was an easy enough shot, but Moses Calhoun had hunted plenty of game in the tall brush and knew well enough that he could not hit what he could not see. So he rose up from behind the trunk of the tree, his long gun clutched in one hand, and he made a dash across to the other side of the draw, hoping to get around to where he could see behind the cluster of boulders.

Another shot echoed off the side of the mountain, and Calhoun heard the bullet zip through the branches not far from him. For just a moment he saw Mullen's head and shoulders above the rocks, but he quickly ducked back down.

Calhoun witnessed Henry Chatham's style of coaxing men out into the open, but he decided now that there'd been too much talking. His interest was to see this thing finished.

He made another run, this time directing his path through a thick stand of fir trees where, on the other side, he would find himself up on the same ridge as Mullen, and not more than thirty-five yards away.

As Calhoun sprang in among the branches of the fir trees, Mullen tried another shot, and then another. The lead balls cut through the branches, whistling dangerously close. Calhoun found his way impeded by the thick branches. He slowed down, and it worried him not to push through faster. A slow target was easier to hit.

Another shot came from the cluster of trees, just as blind as the first four shots, but this one found its target, or damn close. The bullet smashed into Calhoun's canteen, hanging from a strap over his shoulder and cinched to his belt with a leather strap. The lead ball smashed through one side of the canteen and then through the other, though it did not penetrate his leg. But it felt like he'd been smashed in the upper thigh by a ball-peen hammer.

"Damnation," Calhoun swore as he tumbled through the branches and sprawled onto the ground.

He rolled on the ground to examine the wound. It was not so bad – the lead ball, or maybe the jagged edges of the canteen, tore through his trousers and cut his skin, but the lead did not enter the leg. Still, it gave him a terrible, sharp pain, and immediately his leg felt like it had seized up.

Calhoun pushed himself off the ground and tested his leg. It hurt like the devil, but he could move with a limp.

"Did I hit you?" Harlan Mullen shouted.

Ignoring Mullen's taunt, Calhoun pushed through the branches and finished his run, getting to the top of the ridge. He was exposed now, with just a pine tree to provide him cover. And without even looking, he knew he would now have a clear shot at Mullen. He'd run clear of the rocks, and now there was nothing to impede Calhoun from taking a shot at the man.

Mullen scrambled to his feet and did the smart thing. Rather than try to flee, he charged.

Calhoun glanced at the man, saw that Mullen was coming on at a slow run. He was making an odd, lumbering sort of run as he limped forward on his injured leg. Already Calhoun's thumb pulled back the lock on the Poor-Boy rifle. He brought the big gun up to his shoulder, drew a bead on his target, and squeezed the trigger.

The powder flashed in the pan, but the shot did not go.

Misfire!

Harlan Mullen saw the failed attempt and took his chance. With one chamber still loaded, Mullen squeezed the trigger on his Colt Dragoon. But he was running and limping. He did not slow down to take his shot, and his aim was off. The lead ball snapped the air as it passed by Calhoun's head. Mullen was still twenty yards out, but he didn't give up the charge. The thing was started now and would not be easily stopped.

Mullen tossed aside the Colt and produced an Arkansas Toothpick from his belt, a straight-blade fighting knife that Moses Calhoun immediately recognized as having once belonged to Old Eli Simmons.

Now Mullen was just a few feet away, the knife raised up over his head.

Calhoun flipped the big rifle in his hands, and holding it by the barrel, he swung the heavy rifle like a club.

Harlan Mullen leapt at his opponent and Moses Calhoun clubbed him in the ribs with the rifle, batting him away like a fly.

Mullen clattered to the ground, and Moses Calhoun jerked the hatchet from his belt, spreading his legs and squaring his shoulders.

Mullen scrambled up, and for the first time, Calhoun got a clear look at him.

Henry Chatham's shot had caught Harlan Mullen in the back of his hip and ripped a hole clean through him. He was bleeding front and back, and the man was ghostly pale under his stubble-beard. He'd lost a lot of blood and was still bleeding. His trousers were wet and dark.

"Give up, Mullen," Calhoun said. "I ain't here to kill you, but I'll do what I have to."

"Like hell," Mullen said. He wiped a hand across his forehead, rallying himself for another attack. Then he lunged forward, jabbing the Arkansas knife at Calhoun.

Moses Calhoun leaned back to avoid the blade, but at the same time he swung the hatchet, slicing a deep wound in Mullen's upper arm.

Mullen staggered back but then came forward again, slicing with the knife.

Calhoun rolled under the knife, and swung the hatchet again, this time the blade embedded in the muscle on Mullen's thigh. The man was hurt bad now, bleeding even more from his fresh wounds. But he was still unwilling to submit.

Moses Calhoun pushed himself up to his feet, his leg aching, but he knew he had the better of his opponent. Mullen charged one more time with the knife.

Calhoun swung the hatchet again, and this time he caught Mullen in the forearm with the heavy ball side of the weapon. Mullen's arm made a loud snap. The knife flew from his hand, and Mullen fell back again, grabbing his broken arm.

Moses Calhoun kicked the man hard in his wounded hip, and Harlan Mullen fell to the ground with a whimpering yelp.

"It's over, Mullen," Calhoun said. "I'm taking you back now."

With Harlan Mullen still sprawled on the ground, Calhoun put a knee in the man's back and searched him for weapons. He had a small pocket knife that Calhoun tossed away. In the search, Calhoun also found a small purse with coins. He recognized the purse as the one that Eli Simmons had once set down on Calhoun's table back in his cabin.

"This the money you took from the old man back in the town?" Calhoun asked.

Mullen did not give an answer.

Calhoun tucked the purse into his belt and tied it there with the leather cords that cinched it shut.

- 13 -

Moses Calhoun and Aka Ne'ai and Henry Chatham and his prisoners spent the night in Chester Klemp's cabin.

Calhoun could not remember a time when he was so grateful for the warmth of a cabin and a chimney fire.

Chatham offered some mild treatment for Harlan Mullen's injuries, wrapping bandages around his upper arm and thigh.

"Don't matter if it infects, Harlan," Henry Chatham told him. "It's the noose for you, anyway."

"I ain't been tried," Harlan Mullen said.

Chatham grinned at him. "They ain't paying me two hundred dollars a head on you boys without planning to hang you, I can tell you that."

With Calhoun's help, Henry Chatham made a splint for Mullen's broken arm. The man had lost of a lot of blood and was battered and broken. He seemed to hardly have the strength to hold himself upright after the walk back to Chester Klemp's cabin.

They left Mullen and Buddy Carver tied at the wrists and ankles and lying on the floor of Chester's cabin. It seemed a cruelty to tie a man's broken arm behind his back like that, but Calhoun did not object to Chatham for the way he treated his prisoners.

Through the night, Calhoun and Chatham took turns watching the men. Before she turned in for the night, Calhoun gave Aka Ne'ai his Colt Navy so that she would be armed and able to protect herself if the men should get free. Though increasingly, Harlan Mullen did not seem likely to pose a threat to anyone, Calhoun figured there was still some small chance that Buddy Carver might put up a fight to try to get free.

Paul Bentsen's and Slap Duncan's bodies stayed outside, wrapped in sheets. In the morning, they tied the bodies over the backs of their horses, and with the fog still crawling across the mountain forest and down in the valley below, the caravan began its descent into the valley, leaving Chester Klemp to get through the winter on his own.

Aka Ne'ai spoke little through the night, but she stayed close to Moses Calhoun.

"Those men killed my father," she said as they made

their way along the trail leading to the valley.

"I know," Calhoun said.

"They forced me to come with them."

"I know that, too."

"Do you know what happened to my sons?"

"Given to a white family down in the town," Calhoun said. "You'll get them back."

Calhoun did not ask the woman what hardships she endured while she was in the possession of Harlan Mullen and his outfit, nor did he seek to offer her any kind of comfort. A woman such as Aka Ne'ai knew that life could sometimes prove harsh, and she did not desire comfort. She survived a thing that many women might not survive, and that was enough.

The caravan of horses and mules, prisoners and dead, bounty hunter and Snake woman, followed Moses Calhoun along the long path from Chester Klemp's cabin.

They could not simply descend the mountain. The slopes below Chester's cabin featured steep drops and rocky cliff faces falling into deep and impassible canyons, and Moses Calhoun knew that to get off the mountain and down into the valley they would have to make their way back to the south, rounding the east face of the mountain. That would take them back down among the rolling hills and the mountain lake and into the eastern valley where they could return to the town. As much as he did not want to go, Calhoun was resolved to take Aka Ne'ai back to town to be sure that she could collect her children.

Calhoun knew how white Christian women could be, and though he did not know the people who had Aka Ne'ai's children, he suspected that they might balk at giving the boys back to their heathen mother. Perhaps not. But Aka Ne'ai might find that having a white man to speak for her would make some difference.

The sun did little to alleviate the chill in the air. The cold seemed to rise up from the snow-covered ground where it was caught by the gentle wind whisking through the tall pines and spruce trees, and riding on the wind, the cold then permeated everything. It blew up under the brim of Calhoun's hat. It found its way into his coat and under his shirt, and it clenched his bones inside.

He had wrapped a bandage tight around his leg. The wound was small enough, no serious matter, but the bruise and ache where the spent bullet punched his thigh caused him pain when he tried to walk. And here, high up on the mountain with steep slopes and low-hanging branches, the caravan found they had no choice but to walk.

Calhoun eased his pain by leaning against the sorrel horse and allowing the horse to find its way home. A good horse would do that.

Buddy Carver, his face a broken mess and still covered in blood, walked with his hands bound.

Harlan Mullen could not walk any distance, and so Henry Chatham tied him across his horse's back, arms and wrists tied under the horse's belly. Every step the horse took sent waves of pain through his shot side, and Mullen poured forth a stream of curses and whimpers.

Henry Chatham had no pity for the men, and it was clear that the bounty hunter did not care if they lived or died. For Chatham, his prisoners were simply numbers on a bank draft that he would get when he returned them to Denver, and he would get those numbers whether the prisoners arrived whole and healthy or needing an undertaker.

They camped that first night on the mountain side.

Calhoun made shelters for him and Aka Ne'ai.

Henry Chatham erected a tent for the two prisoners, and when they were inside, he bound them fast together with rope so that neither man could move. He forced them to lie back to back – the only consideration being that Mullen did not have to lie on his wounded side – and tied them together at the necks, at the waists, and at the ankles. This was in addition to their wrists, separately bound. The two men lived in a miserable state of exhaustion, weakness, and hunger.

"A hungry man, broken in body and spirit, is less likely to make trouble," Chatham told Moses Calhoun. "I've traveled with prisoners before, and I know how to treat them to keep them subdued."

Calhoun, for his part, found it distasteful. He wouldn't treat an animal he intended to butcher and cook in such a fashion, and it seemed wrong to him to treat men in such a way – killers or not. But these were Chatham's prisoners, and he was the man who was going to have to take them all the way back to Denver.

"How far are we from the valley?" Chatham asked.

They were seated now, hunched over a small cooking fire. Aka Ne'ai, wrapped in a blanket, sat very near to Moses Calhoun, whether for protection or warmth – or maybe both – was hard to say. Calhoun had a pot over the fire, in it a mixture of jerky and flour, sliced carrot and onion, and corn he'd cut from a cob. The appearance wasn't much, but Henry Chatham felt his backbone snatching at his belt buckle and was eager to try the concoction, whatever it tasted like.

"We'll descend the mountain tomorrow and be in the valley by the time we break for camp."

"And from there it is a straight shot through the valley to the town," Chatham said. "Right?"

Calhoun nodded. "Mostly that's right. Through the valley to Ethan Corder's farm," he said. "There is a road from the farm to the town."

"I'll be glad to get back to the town," Chatham said. "It's freezing cold."

Moses Calhoun shrugged his shoulders slightly.

"It gets worse."

"You're coming back to the town with me?" Chatham said. "I'll need your help to bring in these prisoners. They're still dangerous. Every time I have to untie them and move them or get Harlan up on that horse, it's an opportunity for them to try something."

"I'll go all the way to the town," Calhoun said. "But only because I intend to make certain Aka Ne'ai gets her children back."

Henry Chatham laughed.

"I'm sure that reward money doesn't have anything to do with it. You know, you'll have to make your claim on the money with Sheriff Wooten, and then wait for me to get these men back to Denver before you can be paid."

Moses Calhoun shrugged again.

"I'm not worried about the money. I got what I came up here to get."

Chatham squinted his eyes doubtfully.

"Be a helluva lot better for me if I could believe that," he said with a grin. "What did I tell you? Thirty dollars a head? – One hundred and twenty for the lot. That's a mighty large chunk of my cash I promised you. I guess Bentsen don't get his share, but I'll have to give Sheriff Wooten and Irwin their share on Wesley Mullen, I suppose."

Calhoun took a metal bowl and ladled some of the food into it. He handed the bowl to Aka Ne'ai. He gave Chatham a second bowl.

"That's all there is of the carrot and onion," he said. "No more corn, neither. We're on jerky and hardtack the rest of the way unless someone wants to make biscuits with the flour we have."

The ear of corn had been a gift from Chester Klemp, but it was just the one ear and wouldn't travel far.

"We'll make due with what we have," Chatham said. "Yes, sir. Huntin' bounties ain't no easy work, and the more hands you have the less profitable it can be."

Moses Calhoun nodded but did not say anything.

The mountain wilderness offered its own kind of justice. If a man couldn't hack it, he was punished. If a man interfered with another man, that man had the right to stop the interference. These were simple things and made more sense than a man sitting in front of a crowd and arguing his innocence when everyone already knew what he'd done.

Moses Calhoun knew Chester Klemp as a neighbor and friend. Chester had never done him any harm, and whatever Chester had done down below to earn warrants was none of Calhoun's business. But a man like Henry Chatham, who also had no business in it, would come to these mountains and take Chester if he could, and he'd do it all for money. And if he killed Chester, that was a killing that would be forgiven as necessary and earn wages in the towns below. For Moses Calhoun, it was hard to understand how a bounty hunter killing a man was any less a sin than whatever it was Chester had done.

"Those men in the towns below love their rules too much," Calhoun observed.

***

Overnight the clouds returned. The fog never truly lifted from the mountain as the small band made its way lower, and before mid-morning the fog intermingled with pellets of ice and flakes of snow, and the misery for the travelers increased.

"If the snow continues, the valley will be rough traveling," Calhoun observed.

"But passable?" Chatham asked.

"Certainly," Calhoun said. "Passable, but difficult. The horses will object as the snow gets deeper. Impassable, that's when the snow is so high that the buffalo have tunnel their way through the snow, but that kind of snow is still weeks away."

"Tunnel their way?" Chatham repeated. "How do you mean?"

"The bulls or the mamas go out in front, stamping down the snow, pushing it aside with their heads. Tunneling right through it so the calves have a path. It's exhausting work, and will kill a buffalo cow just trying to get her calves to food."

"Kill her?" Chatham said.

"I've seen them drop dead from exhaustion," Calhoun said. "The winter kills more animals out here every year than the big cats or the wolves ever do."

"It's not going to get that deep?" Chatham asked.

"Not this early," Calhoun said. "But we could have a couple of feet of snow before we get home."

The forest floor had only been covered in patches of snow up to now, but even as they descended along the mountain trail, the draws became deep with fresh snow. Branches cracked and broke loose under new weight, the snaps echoing through the trees as branches crashed to the ground.

Aka Ne'ai pulled her blanket tight around her, clutching at her chest.

Calhoun, who preferred not to travel with his heavy bearskin coat, wore it now, alternating between sweating under the coat from the exertion of the hike to freezing when he took it off. As the morning wore into midday, he finally decided to leave off the coat, if for no other reason than because he would be that much warmer when he put it on at nightfall.

Despite the falling snow, Calhoun through the day noted tracks along their path, mostly in the muddy places protected from the snow by the canopy of trees. When he spotted clear tracks, he took the time to examine them.

"What is it?" Chatham asked.

"Tracks," Calhoun said, squatting down beside a muddy spot not yet covered by snow.

"Whose tracks?"

"My guess is that they belong to Bearclaw Jim," Calhoun said. "This is definitely a man's heel here. And this track is a horse, see how it's more round? And this one here, this is a mule. It's more oblong in shape. So I reckon it to be a man leading a horse and mule out of here, probably half a day in front of us. That's got to be Bearclaw Jim."

Chatham stood over Calhoun, examining the tracks for himself. He could not distinguish much difference between the horse track and the mule track, but he accepted that Calhoun probably knew better than him.

"Why would he be on the same path we're on?" Chatham asked.

Calhoun grunted.

"We're not on a path, we're just following the natural lie of the land. He's doing the same thing, and I suppose he's bound for the same place."

"Going back to the town?" Chatham said.

"Nowhere else to go," Calhoun said.

"You don't think he'd try an ambush, do you?"

Calhoun shook his head.

"I wouldn't think so. Bearclaw Jim's only interest is in Bearclaw Jim. He's not the sort who would risk himself to help these others."

They continued along, leading the horses, and after some time, Calhoun glanced back and noticed that Henry Chatham's gaze was fixed upon him, the man's lips twisted as if he was deep in thought. Chatham saw Calhoun notice.

"You're an interesting man, Mr. Calhoun," Chatham said.

"Am I?"

"You're very comfortable in the forest and the mountains," Chatham said. "Not much scares you, does it?"

Calhoun shook his head.

"I've never had much time to be scared, Mr. Chatham," Calhoun said. "A man stays busy enough just making sure he's got wood for the winter and meat in the smokehouse."

"What brought you into these mountains?" Chatham asked. "You on the run from something?"

Calhoun laughed, thinking of Chester Klemp now back up at his cabin, probably filling in the hole in his smokehouse.

"You looking to catch another bounty while you're up here, Mr. Chatham?"

Chatham slipped on an icy rock, catching himself on his horse's lead rope. The horse pulled away, catching Chatham still off-balance, and the man dropped to a seated position in the snow.

"Damned uncomfortable in these woods," he muttered. He still had hold of the lead rope, and he now pulled himself up on that with his horse pulling the other way. Calhoun watched the horse. It was plain to see the animal was irritated with the man, and for a moment Calhoun worried that the horse might buck or rear and kick or try to make a run.

"If we're cold, the horse is cold, too," Calhoun said. "If we're sore and tired, the horse ain't no better. Treat him decent, and he'll return the favor."

Chatham frowned, irritated to be chastised, even mildly. He fancied himself a decent horseman, and didn't care to be talked down to about horses.

Calhoun kept walking and Chatham hurried to catch up. He took a look back at Harlan Mullen, tied over the horse. Mullen wasn't moving, and Chatham wondered if he was dead. Buddy Carver's eyes were bloodshot, dark circles around them against his pale skin. The man looked miserable, which was just exactly how Chatham wanted him to be.

"You didn't answer me," Chatham said. "What brought you into the mountains?"

Calhoun gave a little shrug.

"If it's a bounty you're looking for, I reckon the only person who might be willing to pay for me is my mama, if she's still alive."

"So there's no point taking you back with me," Chatham laughed.

"I'm afraid not," Calhoun said. "No warrants on me."

"So you just came up here because you like snow?" Chatham pressed.

"I reckon I first came because I wanted to see it all for myself," Moses Calhoun said. "I come up on the Yadkin River in the mountains in North Carolina. Little mountains, but pretty enough. You ever hear of Daniel Boone?"

"Sure," Chatham said.

"He was a big name where I was from," Calhoun said. "He lived for a time in those parts, there along the Yadkin. And I guess hearing those stories when I was young gave me a bit of what my daddy would have called the 'wanderings.'"

Calhoun stopped himself. He wasn't a man given to

too much talk, especially if it served no purpose. And yet here he was running off at the mouth.

Chatham waited a moment, and then he prompted Calhoun. "So you just wandered up here?"

"I wandered a bit," he said. "I'd heard about the Rocky Mountains and wanted to see them for myself."

Chatham took a deep breath and watched it fog in front of his face as he let it out.

"Where do your loyalties lie in the war?" Chatham asked.

Calhoun shook his head at the question.

"I ain't in a war, Mr. Chatham," Calhoun said.

"Your state is in a war. Unless it's already over. Last I heard, things wasn't going too good for the Confederates. Back over the summer, they got whipped in Pennsylvania and Mississippi, both."

Calhoun's existence in the mountains was not so removed that he was ignorant of the goings-on back East. He knew of the war, or some of it. He did not know about Pennsylvania nor Mississippi.

Though he kept walking, Calhoun twisted around to face Chatham.

"I don't live in a state, Mr. Chatham," he said. "I live on a mountain. The only soldiers who ever pass by are going to kill Indians. Generally, I disapprove of that war. The Tribe People, they're just like you or me, trying hard to lay up enough to survive the winter. But that's not my fight, neither, so I do what I can to stay out of it. If North Carolina boys are getting killed in Pennsylvania, it doesn't make me want to pick a side. It just makes me wonder at what sorts they have in Raleigh these days."

Chatham chuckled.

"How come you ain't fighting back east, Mr. Chatham?"

Chatham winced at the question. Every man his age who didn't wear a uniform had to have a ready answer for that question, or be prepared to endure the sneers of women and old men.

"I do my part," Chatham said.

"Didn't you say you used to chase fugitive slaves?" Calhoun asked. "I would think you'd have a dog in that fight if anyone did."

Chatham shrugged and wiped a hand across his forehead.

"I ain't a soldier," he said. "When the war started, I came west. Took up in Denver. Got a job as a marshal until I realized the money was in hunting bounties."

Calhoun had never been through Alabama, except on a steamboat on the Tennessee River. He did not know much about the state except that it did not have mountains like these, nor did it experience snow like this. Not that Calhoun had experienced mountains like this in North Carolina, but at least he was accustomed to heavy snows and steep hills.

"I suppose this land is harsh for you," Calhoun said.

"I manage," Chatham said. "But I'd rather be home, if that's what you mean."

As they went along now in silence, Moses Calhoun considered a man who would hunt runaway slaves and fugitive outlaws but was unwilling to fight in an army. He supposed it was a kind of cowardice, though there wasn't much cowardly in one man facing four. But pursuing men in flight gave a certain advantage to the pursuer, and Calhoun guessed that probably Henry Chatham liked having an advantage.

Through the afternoon, the snow fell on the caravan of travelers as they descended down closer to the valley. And then, almost imperceptibly because the thickness of the spruce forest hid the lay of the land, they entered a hollow and climbed out the other side, and ahead of them Calhoun could see the ground level out to nothing more than small hills, the forest opened up – a large stand of white-barked aspen lay in front of them, and beyond that the trees gave way to a meadow blanketed in white. They were at last off the mountain and down in the valley.

"We'll camp here tonight," Calhoun announced. "In the morning we'll start our march through the valley."

- 14 -

Harlan Mullen was not dead, but keeping him alive seemed like it was going to be more difficult.

Despite the tremendous cold, Mullen had taken a fever.

"Probably an infection," Calhoun said.

Short of cutting off a diseased limb, Moses Calhoun couldn't do much for a man who took an infection and a fever. He boiled a tea of pine and cut away the outer layer of bark on an aspen tree to expose the soft bark underneath. That soft bark was both edible and medicinal. Like the tea of a white pine, it could relieve pain and back down a fever, and Calhoun put much stock in the powers of an aspen.

"I doubt it'll do him much good, though," Calhoun said, looking at Harlan Mullen where they'd laid him out under a tent. "Even if we can get him to drink it, he seems a mite far gone for tea to recover him."

Chatham insisted on binding Mullen's wrists and ankles, but at least now he had not forced the man to lie back-to-back with Buddy Carver.

For the present, Chatham had Buddy Carver tied to a tree trunk with a blanket thrown over him. The man's teeth chattered something ferocious, and several times he begged to be let into the tent with a promise that he wouldn't run.

"When you caught runaway slaves, is this how you treated them?" Calhoun asked.

Chatham grinned devilishly.

"Let me tell you something, Mr. Calhoun," he said. "These men may be stomped like a bug right now, but they's as dangerous a pair as you could meet. A man like me don't live long if he's doing favors for such as these. You let ol' Buddy Carver get warm inside a tent, and next thing you know he's thinking about that rope waiting for him at the end of the trail. And then he's thinking up how he's gonna get loose, and what he's going to have to do to you so that he can make his escape. No, sir. It might not be appetizing the way I treat these men, but I plan to see my home again. As for the slaves, they wasn't worth nothing to me if I brought them back in any such way other than fit for work. So, to your question – no, I never did treat the slaves this away."

Paul Bentsen's and Slap Duncan's bodies were frozen so stiff that Calhoun and Chatham had trouble getting them off of the horses.

Burying the bodies was beyond the question. They did not have shovels, and the ground was too frozen to dig into anyway. So Calhoun rigged up a couple of travoises to pull the bodies along behind. They could have never gotten down off the mountain dragging the bodies behind horses, but through the snow-covered meadow, a travois would travel well.

Calhoun made a fire in a clearing among the aspen, and he built it up larger than he might ordinarily do. As a rule, Calhoun preferred a small fire for cooking, and even on the coldest nights didn't trust a fire for warmth. Fire could bring any number of dangers. The smell of food cooking could bring bear or mountain lions. The smell of smoke could bring men – either white men or Indians – and Calhoun knew well enough that a man could prove to be the biggest danger in the forests, on the mountain, and down in the valley. But he made an exception now.

Aka Ne'ai was clearly suffering from the cold, and Henry Chatham's treatment of Buddy Carver was putting that man's life in jeopardy.

So Calhoun built up a fire that would suffice to offer warmth to the woman and the prisoner.

As for Harlan Mullen, he hardly took the tea, and Calhoun did not expect the man to live very far into the eastern valley.

As night fell, Moses Calhoun noted that Chatham had taken more interest in everything he did. Chatham watched over his shoulder as he made the fire, cooked the dinner, even as he built a small shelter for himself and one for Aka Ne'ai. Chatham had tents and did not need to know how to make a shelter, but he watched and even asked questions.

Calhoun slept only a little.

On long hunts, when he was by himself for days at a time, he learned to live with little sleep. Too many predators wandered these forests at night for a man to enjoy the luxury of a deep sleep.

But the night passed with nothing more than a couple of wolves at some distance calling to each other.

In the morning, Calhoun packed his gear with Chatham again watching everything he did.

He left his shelters standing as they were. It was a favor to a man who might find himself lost, exhausted, or injured and in need of a place to bed down, and most of the hunters and trappers did the same.

Chatham took a great interest in Calhoun's doings. He watched closely as Calhoun packed his pannier and loaded it on the mule.

"We'll ride, now, and make better time," Calhoun said. "Just four days, maybe five, we'll be to the other side of this valley."

They could possibly do it in three, but Calhoun knew that a hundred different things could go wrong and delay their trip, and the travoises would slow them a little.

As Calhoun slid his foot into a stirrup and started to step up into the saddle on the sorrel horse, Henry Chatham was standing just a few feet away from him, close enough that Calhoun heard the click of the hammer on the six-shooter.

"Sorry about this, Calhoun," Chatham said, and he pulled the trigger.

***

Later, Moses Calhoun would remember hearing the crack of the shot more than he would remember feeling the impact of the bullet.

Calhoun pitched forward over the horse just as the lead ball struck.

His possibles bag, and its contents, is what saved him. With the bag slung over his shoulder as he climbed into the saddle, he had unconsciously pushed the bag around behind him so that when he heard the cock of the gun and fell forward across the saddle, the bag took the initial impact of the bullet. Its energy spent and its path redirected by those things inside the leather bag, the bullet shot up Calhoun's back without ever penetrating his muscle or organs.

He pitched forward, but when he felt the thud of the ball as it creased his back, Calhoun fell backwards into the snow below him. But he stayed aware. Hearing the hammer on the gun click into a cocked position, Moses Calhoun knew what was coming. The bounty hunter intended to betray him. Had he not heard the hammer cock, he might have been stunned into inaction when the lead ball hit, but he'd been ready for it. He'd thrown himself forward hoping the shot might go high. And when it did not, he kept his head.

His bag hit the snow on the other side of the horse – the lead ball, combined with Calhoun's violent reactions, knocked the bag forward and off his shoulder.

The sorrel horse started and danced in place when Calhoun went down, but Calhoun rolled quickly under the horse's legs, clutching his possibles bag in his hand. He sprang up from the ground at a run.

Aka Ne'ai, witnessing the sudden violence and intuitively understanding that it would lead inevitably to misfortunes for her, wheeled her horse and snapped the reins against the horse's hind quarter. The horse darted among the aspen trees, Aka Ne'ai ducking low branches, and riding like an expert cavalryman.

The six-shooter burst out again, and then a third time. Chatham tried to shoot down the woman, but the horse was cutting between the tall, narrow aspens, and Chatham failed to get a clean shot at the Indian woman. She was good on a horse and rode it well, using her thighs against the horse's side to direct it as it bounded through the forest.

Henry Chatham counted on his first shot being fatal, but Calhoun had pitched himself forward at the last moment and the bullet had hit his bag merely digging a deep groove up his back. Now, instead of Moses Calhoun lying dead on the ground and Chatham in a position to deal with the Indian woman, he had Calhoun running one direction and the Injun riding hard for the mountain slope in another direction.

Seventy yards out, Aka Ne'ai dropped from her saddle and went on foot, running down into the hollow at the far end of the stand of aspens.

Chatham swore. The Indian woman was free and clear. If he was going to kill her, he'd have to turn back, like as not climb half the way back up that mountain, and he wasn't willing to do that.

He stepped out from behind the sorrel horse, looking for Calhoun. But in an instant, the mountain hunter had disappeared into the forest. Henry Chatham spared a glance at the blood in the snow beside the sorrel horse. He couldn't be sure how bad Calhoun was shot, but the man had left a good quantity of his blood.

Buddy Carver was already tied to his horse, and when Chatham drawed down on Calhoun, Buddy didn't quite grasp what was happening. And unlike the Indian woman, Buddy Carver also did not understand what it would mean for him.

He watched in a state of confusion as the Indian woman galloped for safety and Chatham fired two shots that missed her.

And even when Chatham swung the heavy revolver and directed its barrel at him, Buddy Carver still didn't quite understand.

Chatham fired the gun and the bullet smashed square into Carver's chest. His horse started, and Carver fell backwards in the saddle. The rope binding his hands was tied so taut to the saddle horn that he didn't do more than lean in the saddle.

Henry Chatham hurried over to catch the lead rope on Carver's horse before it bolted, and he holstered his gun so that he had both hands free to calm the horse.

Carver's limp body hung grotesquely in the saddle. Chatham cut the rope that held him in place, and the body toppled onto the ground.

Chatham kept a watch for Calhoun, and he moved quickly. He'd already worked out in his mind everything he needed to do, and what he would tell people back in the town when he turned up as the lone survivor from the posse that had gone after Harlan Mullen.

He untied the ropes that held young Paul Bentsen's body on the travois, and then he unceremoniously rolled the body onto the ground. It took some heaving and jerking, but he got Buddy Carver onto Bentsen's travois and quickly tied the body in place.

Then Chatham made a great loop with a rope and looped the leads of all the horses and mules into that. Before stepping into the sorrel's saddle, Chatham took one last look through the aspen trees for Moses Calhoun, but he did not see the man anywhere.

His eyes fell on the horse the Indian woman had ridden away on. It was still standing where she'd left it, seventy yards deeper into the forest.

Chatham swore under his breath. He did not like the idea of leaving that horse behind without knowing for sure that Calhoun's wound was mortal. But it would be more foolish to go back for it and leave the caravan of horses and mules with all the weapons and supplies. So far as Chatham knew, there were no weapons on that horse. Calhoun's long gun was here on the sorrel. There were no provisions – the horse Aka Ne'ai had been riding didn't even have saddlebags. So in the end, Chatham decided he would leave the one horse and get away as fast as possible.

The sorrel did not react well to a strange rider, but Chatham gave the horse a strong kick with his heel, and the sorrel started to move out, leading the pack of horses and mules into the valley.

- 15 -

The cold snow numbed the burning pain down Calhoun's back.

It took a moment to get his breathing under control. He'd come up on the gully without even seeing it, and then he was right at the precipice. He heard shooting behind him, and Calhoun simply dropped down into the gully and fell onto his back, burying the wound into the snow. And the snow that had accumulated in the dry wash was deep.

Calhoun reached for the hatchet on his belt and slid

it from its leather thong, gripping it too tight as the pain burned through him.

He'd been shot, but he could not yet discern how badly he was injured. The pain gripped him like giant fingers, squeezing all the way around his chest, giant fingernails digging into the flesh of his back. His upper back, just below his left shoulder, felt as if someone had struck him with a sledge hammer. Lying in the snow, attempting to feel the extent of his injuries, Calhoun did not know if he would survive.

A panic was rising in his mind. He thought of Kee Kuttai and their children, Elijah and Daniel, and what would they do if he died here in this ditch. The thought worsened the panic – not for himself, but for his children and his wife.

He lowered his grip on the hatchet. He'd known Snake warriors who could throw a hatchet and bury it in a man's chest from fifteen or twenty yards, striking their target ninety-nine of a hundred times. But Calhoun had never been so good with it from distance. He could hit a target closer, but Calhoun's specialty with the hatchet had always been close-in fighting. That would be out of the question now. If Henry Chatham came for him, Calhoun would have to throw the hatchet and trust to his aim. Chatham wouldn't come farther than the lip of that ditch, ten feet above him, and from there he'd fire those Colts and finish Calhoun.

So the mountain hunter laid still in the snow at the bottom of the gully, the hatchet gripped in his hand. He watched the snow falling from gray clouds above, no canopy – or not much of one – to block the snow. The flakes floated and fell in mesmerizing fashion, and Calhoun felt his thoughts beginning to slip into unreality. He tried to focus on the rim of the ditch, watching for the danger he expected to see there. He strained his ears to hear any crunch of snow or snap of twig that might betray his adversary come to finish him off.

But the snowflakes fell in dizzying lines, blending and fading into the clouds above and then reappearing. His eyelids felt heavy. He thought he heard another gunshot, but it seemed far away.

It seemed like just a moment but it could have been half an hour. Calhoun did not remember losing consciousness, but watching the snow fall had left him dizzy.

The hand was warm on his forehead. He'd watched so carefully and listened so closely – or he thought he had – yet somehow Aka Ne'ai had managed to sneak up to him.

"He's gone," she said. Aka Ne'ai had been with the Snake People for most of her adult life, but she had grown up living with Eli Simmons and his Indian wife. When Eli's wife died, he took Aka Ne'ai to live with her mother's people. But she never lost her English in the years she was with the Snake People, married to a chief's son and raising those two boys. Her English words sounded soothing to Moses Calhoun. He liked to hear a woman speaking.

"Chatham?" Calhoun said.

"He rode away with the horses," Aka Ne'ai said. "He shot his other prisoner."

"Shot the prisoner?" Calhoun asked.

He had to focus to make sense of what she was saying. The pain in his back made his mind want to shut down.

"Carver?" he said.

"The one riding the horse," Aka Ne'ai said. "They called him Buddy."

Calhoun took a breath, and the pain cut through his chest.

"How bad are you hurt?" Aka Ne'ai asked.

"You'll have to judge that for yourself," Calhoun said. "Help me to roll over."

Old Eli Simmons' daughter pulled on Calhoun's arm to roll him onto his side, and he clenched his jaw against the pain of her pulling on his arm.

The snow below him was red with blood, and his buckskin shirt slick with it. She had to work to pull his shirt up to see the injury.

"You have a long, deep groove cut into your back," Aka Ne'ai said. Calhoun felt her finger tracing the line of hot pain up his back, and then she stopped. "Oh. It is here. In the muscle."

"What?"

He felt her press against the fleshy part of his back just beside his shoulder blade. She squeezed hard digging at his back with her finger tips, and the pressure sent white hot pain shooting through his shoulder, up his neck and spine, where it burst like an explosion in his head. He thought he would pass out. And then he felt the lead ball roll down his back.

Fresh blood began to spill from the wound.

"I need to bandage this," Aka Ne'ai said.

She took up a handful of snow and pressed it into the wound.

Calhoun's breathing came in short, shallow breaths. The pain from Aka Ne'ai pushing the bullet out of the wound was almost enough to make him pass out.

In his life, he'd broken bones and once had taken a savage swipe from a cougar – and still bore the deep scars from the wound – but he could not remember a time when blinding pain shot so thoroughly through his body. But the cold snow the woman packed into the wound began to numb his shoulder a bit, and Calhoun found he was able to level out his breathing some.

"Help me sit up," Calhoun said after a moment. Aka Ne'ai braced herself and pushed against Calhoun's good shoulder, and with a grunt and some effort, the two of them got him upright.

The grip of his Bowie knife was digging into his stomach as he sat on the ground in the ditch, and he pulled the knife and scabbard off of his belt.

Aka Ne'ai picked up the knife and then slid out of her own wool coat. She laid out the coat, and from the bottom of it she cut several long strips.

"Bandages," she said.

When she was finished cutting the strips from the bottom of her coat, she put what was left of her coat back on. It looked absurd, hanging at her midriff, but it still served to give her some warmth.

"I will come right back," she said.

Aka Ne'ai, Calhoun's knife still in her hand, followed the ditch a little ways to where it rose up some, and then climbed out of the gully. She was gone for some time, the bandages still laid out in the snow beside Calhoun. He could feel the wound on his back still bleeding, though he did not think the blood was freely flowing in a way that might prove immediately dangerous.

The Snake woman hurried out of the grove of aspen toward the rich, green spruce trees surrounding the white-barked aspen.

She moved quickly from tree to tree, searching for pieces of dried pitch clinging to the trunks of the spruce trees, and she chipped away the pitch with Calhoun's knife, dropping the pieces into a fold she made in her shirt.

When she had a sufficient amount of the dried sap, she found a flat rock in a small, clear spot where the treetops had prevented the snow from building up too much. She swept the snow and dirt from the top of the rock and emptied the fold of her shirt onto the rock. Then she collected what dry wood she could find, and in the clearing, around the flat rock, she stacked small pieces of kindling. Then she went back to Calhoun.

He'd managed to remain upright while he waited for her to return. His breathing was leveled out, but the pain made him sweat, and the sweat seemed to be freezing him where he sat.

"I need to start a fire," Aka Ne'ai said.

"In the bag," Calhoun said. "I have a char box and flint."

"Butter?" she asked.

Calhoun chuckled in spite of the pain.

"I carry a great many things in my possibles bag, but no butter."

"I need butter or honey, some sort of oil. Anything like that."

"Honey," Calhoun said. "I have a small tin of honey."

"Can you walk up yonder, out of the gully?" Aka Ne'ai asked.

Calhoun twisted to look behind him where the ditch rose and the embankment was shallow, and he felt the sting in his back as he turned. He was in a terrible state of pain, and he knew the wound on his back was still leaking blood out of him.

"I can walk up there," he said through gritted teeth.

Aka Ne'ai nodded. She took up his possibles bag where he had dropped it when he fell down into the gully. She got the strips of bandage that she had cut from her own coat, and then she started up above the lip of the gully.

"I am going to start a fire," she said. "Come up when you can."

***

Calhoun's desire for warmth overcame the pain. It took some effort, but when he smelled the smoke and heard the crackling of a fire, he managed to get up to his feet and make his way along the ditch until it rose to meet the ground above and he could get over the lip without too much difficulty.

Aka Ne'ai had a good fire going in short time. She built the fire up around the rock in the center and had now mixed the spruce pitch into the honey in Calhoun's tin. The tin sat on the rock in the center of the fire.

"The spruce pitch will help it heal," Aka Ne'ai said. "The honey will keep the bandages from sticking to the pitch and the wound."

Calhoun nodded. He knew the remedies used by the Snake People. He'd boiled spruce pitch with butter to apply to wounds in the past.

While the fire cooked the concoction, Aka Ne'ai walked back through the stand of aspen trees, passing among the white-bark trees, all with their black scars. Calhoun took his breaths slowly. The pain in his back grew worse when he breathed in, and he'd found that the more shallow the breaths he took the easier the pain. After several minutes, Aka Ne'ai came back through the stand of trees, leading the horse she'd been riding. She tied the horse nearby to them.

When the honey and pitch combination was boiled down, Aka Ne'ai took the tin from the fire, using the folds of her shirt to grab hold of it without burning her hand. She set the tin down in a patch of snow where it would cool quickly. She packed snow up around the tin and used Calhoun's knife to stir the contents.

"It will not take long now," she said.

Pain has a way of subsiding. A person grows accustomed to pain so that it becomes sufferable. Calhoun chewed his lip for a while and controlled his breathing, but now he found that the pain in his back had diminished. He couldn't raise up his left arm. Using those muscles in his back was too much. But as long as he held his arm clutched to his body, he could manage to walk.

"What do you intend to do?" Aka Ne'ai asked without taking her eyes off the mixture in the tin.

"I'm going after him," Calhoun said, his anger audible in his low tone. "The man shot me in the back and stole my horse. I intend to get back my horse."

"You'll take my horse?" Aka Ne'ai said.

"I'll have to," Calhoun said. "And that six-shooter I gave you."

Aka Ne'ai nodded.

"You'll kill him?" Aka Ne'ai asked.

Calhoun clenched his jaw as he considered it. He believed what he said to Chester Klemp about revenge, but his anger proved difficult to contain.

"I reckon I will," Calhoun said, though he did not like the idea of setting out with the intention of killing a man. Calhoun opposed the thought of revenge. Nothing good came from it. But Henry Chatham had stolen his horse, and Moses Calhoun did not think the man would return it willingly.

"What about me?" Aka Ne'ai said, though she thought she already knew the answer.

"You'll have to make your way back to Chester Klemp's cabin."

"I cannot stay there with him through the winter," she said. "I must get back to my sons."

Calhoun twisted his lips thoughtfully. He couldn't argue with her on that. Those two sons of hers were half the reason Calhoun rode along to save her from Harlan Mullen and his outfit. Calhoun knew that those boys needed their mother. The folks in the town meant well, but giving those boys to a white family wasn't what the boys needed. They'd lost their father and their grandfather in the space of a year, and they needed their mother.

"You can ask Chester to get you back to the town," Calhoun said. "He might do that."

Aka Ne'ai, who did not speak much but heard and

understood everything, narrowed her eyes.

"A wanted man who just had a bounty hunter spend the night in his cabin isn't going to want to take me to the town," Aka Ne'ai said.

"That could be," Calhoun acknowledged. "But you can't come with me."

Aka Ne'ai took that in, stirring the pitch and honey in the tin. She dipped a finger into the syrup.

"It's ready," she said.

Calhoun could not take his shirt off over his head, and Aka Ne'ai had to help him with it. The cold stung his entire body and he shivered without control. He wished he had been wearing his heavy coat when he was shot. There was small chance he could catch Henry Chatham before dark, and he'd find it powerful cold come nightfall.

Aka Ne'ai used snow to clean the wound again, and then she used her fingers to smear her medicinal concoction into the graze wound and the place where the lead ball had buried into Calhoun's shoulder.

"The ball stuck in the muscle," Aka Ne'ai said, examining the wound as she pushed the salve into it. "You are very lucky. It might have hit bone and shattered the bone in your shoulder, or cut right through the muscle. But it stuck right there."

She pressed deep into the wound on Calhoun's shoulder, and he winced at the explosion of white heat in his brain.

"Right there," Aka Ne'ai said again, and Calhoun thought she was digging in his wound again. "That's where it stuck."

He felt her picking at the wound, pain like lightning

flashed up his neck and into his head – blinding pain as the woman dug her fingers into his injured shoulder. He winced and jerked away, but her fingers trailed with him and her other hand pushed on his back, and she leaned her weight into him to keep him from moving.

"Look at this," Aka Ne'ai said.

Calhoun thought he would throw up from the pain, but then, like waves pulling back into the sea, the pain rolled away and eased just a touch, and Aka Ne'ai was holding something out in front of him. Aka Ne'ai's fingers were scarlet with his blood, but between her thumb and forefinger she held a thick piece of leather that she'd dug from his back.

Calhoun narrowed his eyes at it, and he realized it was a piece of leather from his possibles bag.

"You're very lucky," Aka Ne'ai said. "Shot in the leg. Shot in the back. Still not dead. Maybe you should quit before your luck runs out."

"Are you finished with the wound?" Calhoun asked.

"Not yet," Aka Ne'ai said. She tossed the piece of leather onto the ground where Calhoun could see it, and then she went back to smearing the mixture into the wound.

When she had finished, Aka Ne'ai took the bandages she had cut earlier and tied them around Calhoun's chest, layering them in over-lapping fashion on the wound. She tied them tight, almost so tight as to make it difficult for Moses Calhoun to breathe. Then she wrapped a couple of the bandages over his shoulder and under his arm, also tying those tight.

When the bandages were tied, she helped Calhoun get his shirt back on.

With one last bandage, she tied a sling and made Calhoun put his forearm through it.

"Don't move the arm more than you have to," she warned him. "As soon as you can, change these bandages. The wound is still oozing, and if you do not change the bandages and clean it, it will turn bad."

Calhoun nodded his thanks to her.

"I'm obliged to you," he said. "I hate to leave you on your own, but if you move fast, you can make Chester's cabin before night."

Aka Ne'ai frowned.

"Small chance of that," she said.

"Take my bag," Calhoun said, holding out the possibles bag. "You've got my char box and can make a fire to keep yourself warm tonight. And my knife, too. Take that for protection."

He felt guilty leaving her on her own. He was taking her horse and the only gun they had between them. But she was Eli Simmons' daughter, and a Snake woman, and Calhoun knew she could survive a night on her own out here.

"Are you so determined that I cannot talk you out of this?" Aka Ne'ai asked.

"I am so determined," Calhoun said.

Aka Ne'ai nodded, resigned to the notion that she had a difficult day and night ahead of her.

"I hope I see you again," she said.

"If I can catch him quickly, I'll come back for you to see that you get back to town," Calhoun said.

Aka Ne'ai gave a small shrug.

"Perhaps Mr. Klemp will take me," she said.

Before parting ways with her, Calhoun unceremoniously took Bentsen's coat from his body and gave it to Aka Ne'ai. She'd cut so much from her coat that it would hardly serve to keep her warm. Bentsen's coat was too small for Calhoun, anyway, but large enough that Aka Ne'ai could slide it on her over her own coat. Possibly, Bentsen's coat would make the difference between life and death for her as she tried to survive the night on her own.

- 16 -

Moses Calhoun did not know which horse he had. It was a dark bay gelding with black mane and tail, and might have been one of those used by Harlan Mullen's outfit, or maybe it was one that had come with Sheriff Wooten's group from town. Regardless, the horse proved to be a good mount. He didn't much mind the snow, and Calhoun had to rein him in to keep him from starting out through the valley at a gallop.

"We've got a long way to go," Calhoun told the horse. "No sense in using yourself up before we've gotten far."

The breeze through the meadow bit down to the
bone. The hole in his deerskin shirt allowed the cold air
to circulate around him. His bandages soon felt icy. His
back was wet with blood and the snow Aka Ne'ai had
used to clean his wound. Up on the horse, there was no
escaping the frigid cold. The gray clouds above continued
to spread snow over the valley, but Calhoun believed it
was now falling lighter than it had been. He ached,
though, for the sun to show itself and give him some kind
of warmth. He'd been through this valley plenty of times
when the snow covered the ground and the breeze blew
chilly, but the sun overhead warmed his face and hands.
He was desperate now for that warmth.

But the snow was not coming so fast now that it
would cover Henry Chatham's tracks. Chatham was
leading a train of horses and mules, and dragging two
travoises along with him, and he'd cut a trail that a blind
man could follow.

With one arm in a sling and the other holding the
reins, Calhoun used his legs to direct the horse into the
deep ruts in the snow left by the travoises and the
animals Chatham had with him. Those ruts were deep
enough to expose the grass below and give Calhoun
confidence that his horse wouldn't step in a hole and go
lame. That confidence allowed the horse to keep a good
pace, a pace faster than anything Henry Chatham was
doing.

As he rode along, deeper into the gray and white
landscape, Calhoun watched for any sign up ahead of him
that he was catching up to Chatham. The last thing he
wanted was to ride so close that Chatham would see him
coming. Calhoun already had a dozen disadvantages
weighing him down – not the least of which was no rifle.
If he had his old Poor-Boy rifle, he might shoot Chatham

from a distance and be done with this thing. But that was now out of the question. So if surprise was going to be his ally, his attack would almost surely have to come after dark.

Calhoun occupied his mind deliberately.

The cold eating at him the way it was, he knew it would be easy to drift off to sleep, to topple from the horse, and find himself another victim of the winter like the buffalo who tunneled through the snow or the otter who wandered too far from a stream and into the path of a coyote.

He thought about his family – the boys chopping kindling, Kee Kuttai making up a stew. She sometimes made dumplings with a venison roast, potatoes and carrots. But there wasn't much better than Kee Kuttai's biscuits and sawmill gravy with chunks of sausage the size of a coat button.

His mind went from food to the warmth of the cabin. Calhoun thought of the days he'd spent chopping wood in the warmth of summer, the sweat covering him like a bath. He kept a pile of chopped wood between two trees a little ways from the cabin. That was the wood seasoning for next winter. The wood to get them through this winter was stacked around the house, up to the windows. He take from the dry wood under the porch roof first, and as those stacks began to diminish, he'd get the wood from around the sides of the cabin to replenish the stacks under the porch roof. Laziness would make him leave the wood around back until last.

If the winter proved long or particularly cold and they went through all of the wood stacked around the house, he had some under a canvas tarp that he could get to, even if the snow stayed high. But he'd not yet encountered a winter that was so long that he ever had to get too deep into that pile.

The cabin got so warm at times that they would sometimes have to crack open the windows to allow in some cold air to balance out the temperature. But those windows would never stay open for long.

In the harshest weeks of winter, the family would sleep in the loft under blankets and bearskins, Daniel and Elijah sleeping up in the loft between their parents. The loft stayed warm with the heat from the fire rising up into the gable. These were pleasant times when they might all sleep in a little late, snuggled under the blankets like a family of bears gone in for the winter.

Thinking of the warmth of his cabin proved to be the wrong line.

Calhoun felt his eyelids growing heavy as his mind blocked out the cold all around him, and he realized he was leaning heavy in the saddle.

He straightened himself up now, getting his seat again, and shifted his thinking.

From the time Henry Chatham left him for dead to the moment Calhoun set off in pursuit, probably not more than two hours had passed.

That was quite a lead Chatham had, but in this snow – and trailing a caravan of horses and mules – Chatham could not travel fast. Calhoun tried to work out in his mind how long it would take him to catch Chatham.

With a cleared path, Calhoun could move a good bit faster than Chatham. But Chatham also wasn't the sort who would likely worry overmuch about the condition of his horses. He might run those horses ragged, or not care if one of them broke a leg in a hole hidden under the snow. He would travel faster than he should, but if he ran one of those horses into the ground, that would also slow him down.

With some luck, Calhoun thought he might see Henry Chatham before dark.

And then it would be an issue of following him without being seen. The valley floor was lined by forests where the big spruce and fir forests dropped down off the surrounding mountains and into the valley. Calhoun might ride in among the trees and follow unseen, and then at dusk he could sneak up close to whatever camp Chatham made and take him in the dark. Chatham was the sort of man who would make a big fire, and that would be an advantage for Calhoun.

A small enough advantage, considering all else that was against him.

He'd lost blood and felt weak. He could take his arm out of the sling, but the injury to his back had left the arm all but useless. The cold was also working against him. His limbs were growing numb. His face stung it was so cold. His teeth were chattering so that he had to work to make them stop.

As he rode along, searching the horizon for Henry Chatham, Moses Calhoun began to wonder if he'd made a terrible decision.

There in the warmth of Aka Ne'ai's fire, going after Chatham seemed obvious. The man stole his horse. The man shot him in the back.

Calhoun's instincts told him he must go and get his horse back, and though he did not like to admit it, he knew deep down that he hoped Chatham would put up a fight. He wanted a chance at the man who shot him in the back.

But now he was beginning to doubt the wisdom in this pursuit.

Even as the doubts began to grip him, up ahead Calhoun saw something in the grayness and the snow. It took the form of a dark shadow.

Calhoun leaned back in his saddle just a touch and gave the reins a slight tug. The bay horse slowed its pace but did not stop. The shadow ahead of him still moved in the grayness. It had to be Henry Chatham and his train of animals.

Certain of what he'd seen in front of him, Calhoun touched the bay gelding's side and led the horse off the trail created by Henry Chatham's caravan, and he rode toward the spruce forest to the south. He could follow Chatham from the tree line. He would be less conspicuous there and better able to use the last of his meager advantages – surprise.

***

The gray day turned grayer with the sun falling below Chester Klemp's mountain at their backs.

Moses Calhoun had picked his was silently through the spruce trees. The spruce gave way to a cluster of aspen, and then Calhoun picked his way silently through the aspen. A man couldn't help but enjoy a ride through an aspen forest, with the tall trees always gently swaying, the white bark of the aspen, scarred black in spots up the trunk, it contained a beauty all its own. A man didn't often think of tree bark as being a thing of beauty, but the aspen trees, even in recession, managed to exude the beauty of their nature. In spring the early shoots of the aspen seemed to glow with the newness of life, a golden green of promise as the snow faded from the land and the mountains and valleys woke and shook the cold months from them. In the summer, a stand of aspen stood out bright and lively from the surrounding spruce trees, shimmering with glee against the stately green of the tall spruce and pines. In the fall, when the leaves turned a brilliant yellow, a stand of aspen looked like a bold statement of beautiful defiance against the winter hardships to come.

And even now, in the grayness of winter, with the clouds hanging low and the snow threatening to cover everything and freeze all that it touched, the aspens offered a proud beauty with their thin trunks and naked branches holding a layer of snow – stark and white, a frozen jewel.

But more than their beauty, aspens held the secrets to survival within their layer of white bark. Boiled, the inner bark made a tasty meal. Its tea was medicinal, relieving pain and even curing infection. A stand of aspen might mean the difference between life and death for a man struggling to survive.

And Moses Calhoun, as he weaved in between the tall trunks, realized now that he was a man struggling to survive.

Feeling the weight of it, he took his hat off his head and slapped it against his thigh to knock away the snow that had collected on its brim.

He had lost sight of Henry Chatham a ways back. He put it down to the falling sun, and the coming darkness from the east, but with no sign of him for half an hour now, Calhoun worried that perhaps Chatham had turned into the trees to the north end of the meadow to make his camp for the night. If he had done so, then Calhoun had ridden right past him and was now out in front.

But even as he considered turning back to try to pick up the trail again, through the tall trunks of the aspen, Calhoun now caught sight of the horses gathered around in a tight circle just at the edge of the aspen forest. He quickly drew reins to stop the bay gelding.

"Whoa," he whispered.

And then he tried to lift his leg to swing it over the horse and get down out of the saddle, but Calhoun found his leg was too stiff to easily move.

He took a breath.

The shot he'd taken to the leg from Harlan Mullen's six-shooter was not a bad wound, but it had left his thigh terribly bruised and painful. In the cold, the entire leg had seized up, numb and stiff.

His back was worse. The bandages did a mite bit to help, but the pain in twisting his body to swing out of the saddle brought water to his eyes.

Moses Calhoun felt like he was probably dying, and he knew he needed warmth and nourishment or he might not last the night.

He took a deep breath, clenching his jaw against the pain that he knew would shoot through his back and the dull ache that would turn to sharp pain when he swung his leg over the saddle, and then he did those things he had to do.

He broke the stiffness in his leg and swung it behind him.

He twisted his back and felt the pain shoot through him.

And he exhaled his breath when his feet were on the ground. He leaned against the horse, grateful that it was not one of those skittish beasts that dances around when a rider dismounts.

If he survived this, he might keep this bay gelding, considering it the spoils of war.

Now he walked the horse back a little ways where it would not be seen, and if it neighed or snorted, he would not be heard. Walking was difficult and painful, but he had the horse to lean against. The horse's breath was hot against his neck and shoulder as they walked along side-by-side, and the couple of times that Calhoun stumbled, the horse seemed to catch him with its muzzle.

He had always been grateful for the warm breath of a horse against him, that warm breath seemed to signify a kind of friendship.

"You wait here," Calhoun said to the horse, tying the reins to an aspen trunk. "If things go well, maybe I'll have you back among your friends shortly."

He did not say what would happen to the horse if things did not go well. Chatham would not think to look for the horse, and it would stay here, tied to the aspen, and likely freeze to death tied to this tree.

Now Calhoun took a few tentative steps. Not having the horse for support made him feel even more unsteady.

He took a few more steps, trying to get the numbness to leave his legs. He stamped his feet a few times, feeling the pins and needles pricking him. His feet were especially cold, and the soles stung worse than his back when he drove them to the ground. He hugged his good arm tight against his body, rubbing his injured arm and shoulder to try to get the blood flowing, tucking his good arm to where he could rub it with his other arm still in its sling. He had to get the blood flowing again in his body, wake up his limbs so that they would be ready for action.

He walked another circle and then went up and slid the Colt Navy six-shooter from the saddle. He checked the percussion caps on the gun to be sure they were still in place. All this riding was the sort of thing that would knock them loose. But the gun was armed with five full chambers and five percussion caps. The sixth chamber, the one the hammer sat on, was empty.

Every bit of his body seemed to be full of pain – either from injuries or stiffness or the numbness of the cold.

What drove him on was the promise of finding among his things the heavy bearskin coat. Food would be nice. A fire, too. But that coat right now seemed to possess the promise of life-giving warmth.

He was unsteady on his feet, and still stiff. But Calhoun knew he could not wait. He would only grow weaker the longer he waited. So he set off in a direction that would take him deeper through the stand of aspen and around to the east side of Chatham's camp. If Chatham was watching for trouble, he'd be watching over his shoulder to the west.

- 17 -

Henry Chatham made quick work collecting firewood from around the aspens. Even before he started to put up his tent, before he unburdened the horses and mules, he started a fire going.

He wore thick, leather gloves, but they were insufficient against the cold he'd been riding through all afternoon. His hands felt frozen. His legs were frozen. His feet were frozen. His nose was frozen. Henry Chatham was as miserable as he could ever remember being.

Alabama didn't have winters like this – even in the

worst of the winter – and this wasn't even bad yet for these mountains.

He just wanted to be done with these mountains, with this terrible, long valley that stretched on forever.

What had Calhoun said? It would take them four days to get back to the town. He had three more days of riding like this in front of him.

He'd occupied his mind with the story he would tell when he got back to town. Most of it was based in truth.

Poor young Paul Bentsen had been shot dead in a shootout with the gang.

Harlan Mullen came out the worst for it in a fight. He'd tell them that fight was between him and Harlan and would not mention Moses Calhoun's involvement. He would say that Buddy Carver was taken prisoner and tried to make an escape, shooting Moses Calhoun in the back before Chatham could gun down Carver. If anyone ever looked for evidence, what they might find would line up well enough with Chatham's lies.

As he'd expected, Harlan Mullen had died on the trail that day. The first thing he did when he dismounted, even before collecting firewood, was check on Mullen. The man wasn't going to survive this journey, not in the way he was. A couple of times earlier in the day he'd made some noises, pleas for help, moaning and whatnot. Chatham left those ignored. He was just waiting for Mullen to expire.

Dead or alive. That's what the bounties out of Denver said about Mullen and his gang.

They could paint this valley floor in blood for all the killing. Slap Duncan and Harlan Mullen, Buddy Carver, Moses Calhoun. Hell, the Injun woman would probably die, too. She was the one loose end that Henry Chatham regretted. She was quick to make an escape. He would have liked to have shot her dead and be certain of her. But even if she did, somehow, survive the cold out here all alone and make it back to town, Chatham would be well on his way to Denver to collect his earnings, and like as not no one would believe an Indian woman's story of Chatham's betrayal.

He might even leave Sheriff Wooten with some story to plant the seeds of doubt. He might say he'd had his way with her and she'd run off.

No one would blame him for using an Indian woman to keep himself warm at night, and if she came into town with stories of Henry Chatham shooting Moses Calhoun in the back, well, Sheriff Wooten and everyone else would just guess that was her way of trying to get revenge on Chatham for how he'd handled her.

All that would sound good in the town.

If they ever did find the bodies and start to figure that things had gone differently from the way Chatham told it, that wouldn't matter. By then he'd have collected his bounty in Denver.

Two-hundred dollars a head for Harlan Mullen's outfit.

It was a fortune, and he wouldn't have to split it with anyone. He might send forty dollars back up for Sheriff Wooten and that fellow Irwin to split for their part in taking Wesley Mullen. But he'd still be left with seven-hundred and sixty dollars.

That was money enough to set him up nice somewhere warmer.

Maybe California. Nobody was fighting in California,

so far as Chatham knew. Most all the fighting was back East. California or New Mexico Territory, somewhere that he didn't have to worry about snow up to his knees.

Chatham got the fire going pretty good, though it was not an easy task. All the wood was wet, but once he got some small twigs going, it was easy enough to add bigger sticks to the fire and let them sizzle and dry out in the flames. He liked a big fire that put off a lot of heat. He considered Calhoun something of a scaredy, old eccentric for the way he preferred small fires.

When the fire was going large enough to take care of itself for a little while, Chatham went to the horses and mules and removed saddles and the travoises and the panniers.

It was laborious work that he despised having to do. Several times, he interrupted it by returning to the fire to throw another branch on.

The animals were all surly from the cold, and so they pushed on him with their muzzles and nipped at him and danced around while he tried to remove their burdens.

He'd never developed a fondness for horses. They were a tool, like a gun or a Blood Hound or a pair of boots. But unlike a hammer or a saw, horses were expensive. Expensive to stall in a barn, expensive to feed, expensive to shoe, expensive to let from the livery stable. Henry Chatham liked to think of himself as an economical man, and he worked hard to avoid costs and increase earnings wherever he could. Horses, too often, sapped profits, but they were an unavoidable cost of doing business.

So he went about the work of unburdening the animals with the bitterness of a man who only valued their worth in dollars and cents.

Soon the only light that shone in the valley was the fire that Chatham had built up at the edge of the aspen trees, and he marveled at how bright the fire glowed out into the valley.

He'd been carelessly throwing on another branch while he worked with the animals, unaware of how overgrown his fire was becoming because he was so bothered by his work. The flames leapt four or five feet into the air and created a circle of light that extended beyond where the horses were tied, and lit the snow on the meadow in an eerie, orange incandescence that flickered and cast long shadows into the empty meadow.

Now, for the first time, he understood Moses Calhoun's cautions against a big fire.

If a band of Injuns or a curious trapper were on the hills opposite, they would see that fire from miles away.

The fire crackled and popped as Henry Chatham crunched through the snow back to stand near it.

Well, he'd made up this big, and there was not a thing he could do about that now. So he might as well enjoy the warmth of it.

All this snow and cold, it seemed unlikely to Chatham that there might be anything – person or animal – wandering close enough to see his fire.

***

Moses Calhoun understood as he softly planted one boot in front of the other that he was sneaking up on death in this valley.

This would not end in any other way. As sure as the

wolves hunted their prey for survival or the big cats stalked for their very existence, as sure as the bears chased away the coyotes from a buffalo carcass so that they might subsist and live another day, Moses Calhoun also stalked his quarry so that he might live through the night.

Calhoun was hurt and weak, hungry and cold.

All of his possessions that he needed to survive were under the control of Henry Chatham, a man who had tried to kill him by shooting him in the back. As he moved silently through the snow-covered aspen forest, stepping from behind one tree trunk to the next, Calhoun understood that one of the two of them would have to die if the other was to survive. This could not be a fight where one merely bested the other and the beat man surrendered.

If Henry Chatham proved victorious, he would finish the job he'd started that morning.

If Moses Calhoun was going to get the warmth and food he needed to live, he would have to kill Henry Chatham.

This valley had been drenched in blood many times.

The blood of the buffalo, the blood of the otter, the blood of the elk and deer, the blood of the big cats and the big bears – the grizz and the black bear – the blood of the Indian and the blood of the white man – in the name of survival, all who came here and called this place home had shed blood on the floor of this valley and on the sides of these mountains. Nature was too harsh for it to be any other way. Life was too harsh for it to be any other way.

As he neared the camp, Calhoun kept his eyes on the growing fire. He watched Chatham working with the animals, removing saddles and panniers, sliding the travoises with the bodies away. As he worked, he kept returning to the fire to toss on another big branch or a handful of sticks. And soon the fire was raging.

Just looking at it made Calhoun feel a little warmer. He imagined that he could feel the heat radiating from that fire out through the aspens, across the floor of the valley meadow.

The thought passed through his mind that when he killed Henry Chatham, he would not kick down the fire. Instead, he would find his bearskin coat among his other belongings, and then he would stand by that fire and warm himself.

He crouched low to the ground, half hidden behind the trunk of a narrow aspen. The aspen trees, for all their beauty and usefulness, were impractical as hiding positions. Even standing sideways, a man of reasonable size standing behind an aspen hung out in front and back. But with his eyes adjusted to the fire, Henry Chatham was unlikely to see Calhoun until the two men were within a few feet of each other.

Now he stood up, bracing himself against the tree, and he took another step. He pushed his toes into the snow, making as little noise as possible, then shifted his weight to put the next foot forward, slowly and softly into the snow.

He tip-toed like this through the snow and bed of leaves, keeping an eye on Chatham the entire way. At some point, he slid his arm out of the sling Aka Ne'ai had tied and pulled the sling over his head, dropping it silently on the ground.

When Chatham was working with the animals, Calhoun moved a bit faster.

When he returned to the fire to warm himself for a moment, Calhoun kneeled down low behind an aspen tree and waited.

Doing so, he managed to get within about ten feet of the perimeter of the camp.

And then Chatham came back to the fire, and Calhoun lowered himself and stayed still.

Chatham was toting supplies – a pot and pan, a sack with some foodstuffs and a sack of flour.

Both arms were burdened with the items Chatham needed to make himself supper. His two Colt pistols were still on his belt, but he wouldn't be able to draw either of them very fast.

Now was the best, easiest chance that Moses Calhoun was going to get.

Calhoun stood up slowly, using the aspen to support himself.

He drew from his belt the Colt Navy six-shooter, a gun he'd taken off a white soldier a year before. He'd kept the gun, assuming it would be useful for protection, if not for hunting. He thumbed back the hammer on the gun and forced his breathing to become calm and easy. The pain of his injuries, the cold and weakness, the exhaustion that seemed to permeate his body – all these things had made the work of sneaking through the aspens very difficult for him and his chest was heaving with the exertion.

But with his breathing calm, Calhoun was ready.

In the name of survival, Moses Calhoun had shot dozens of animals over the years. He always prayed a prayer of thanks for the life they gave so that he and his family might keep their own. This – however this was going to turn out – this was no different.

One last easy inhale. He had to breathe through his mouth because his nose was frozen shut.

And then the mountain hunter stepped out from behind the aspen tree. He took just a few long strides. His feet crunched in the snow, but he no longer worried over that. His prey was in front of him.

Henry Chatham craned his neck to peer at the noise in the woods, and it was too late when he saw Moses Calhoun step out of the darkness, into the circle of fire and within the campsite.

Calhoun had the Colt Navy raised up in front of him, the barrel staring dangerously back at Henry Chatham.

And Chatham, like some damn woman, had his arms full of ingredients.

- 18 -

"Don't drop those things," Calhoun said. His voice came out strong and clear and did not betray the hurt and weakness he felt.

In the flash of a thought, Chatham wondered where Calhoun had gotten the gun from, not knowing that Calhoun had given the gun to Aka Ne'ai to protect herself. But it was only a passing thought. Henry Chatham knew that the thing that mattered was not where Calhoun had obtained the weapon, but instead the thing that mattered was what Calhoun intended to do with it.

"You have me, sir," Henry Chatham said, his rich Southern twang more prominent now. "I am your prisoner."

Calhoun narrowed his eyes. Killing a man in cold blood was something he'd never done before. As much as he'd told himself this was merely survival, like shooting an elk for meat to live through the winter, now that he was at the precipice of the thing, he balked.

"I don't reckon I'm looking for a prisoner," Calhoun said. He took a step forward, wanting to be sure of his aim.

"No, I suppose not," Chatham said. "Once a man shoots you in the back, you probably ain't too inclined to let him live."

Calhoun heaved out a breath and squeezed the trigger on the Colt Navy.

The hammer fell with a soft click, and Henry Chatham winced and shrugged a shoulder up to protect himself.

And in the deafening silence, where the impotent click of the hammer seemed to echo from every mountain, the two men stood for the beat of a heart, both realizing this had not gone the way either of them thought it would. A misfire. A lost cap, or maybe a dud, or it could even be the powder got wet when Calhoun loaded it.

Calhoun reacted first. He never shifted the gun's aim, and he thumbed back the hammer quickly and squeezed the trigger without any hesitation.

Now the gun exploded, but Henry Chatham had made himself small behind his parcels, and the ball shot into the cast iron skillet and disintegrated into oblivion.

Henry Chatham threw up his arms, tossing pot and pan, bacon and flour, all into the air toward Moses Calhoun.

Calhoun threw up an arm and ducked away from the things flying at him, batting away the tin pot that was headed for his head. He cocked back the hammer on the Navy revolver again.

Now Chatham was running. Calhoun had expected him to go for his guns, but Chatham wasn't interested in a stand-up fight.

Chatham dashed around the fire and out into the open meadow.

He was only fifteen or twenty feet away when Calhoun fired the gun again, and this time the ball struck its target.

Chatham took the shot in the lower back, and he pitched forward into the snow. Chatham let out a ragged yell as he went down.

It was a good, clean shot. Calhoun was sure of that. He'd shot at too many animals over the years not to know when he'd had a good shot on one.

But he could see Henry Chatham beyond the fire, out in the open meadow, moving around quickly.

Calhoun stepped away from the fire, as much as he didn't want to. The brief moments of warmth he'd enjoyed being near the fire had felt like life coming back to him, and leaving it now took more discipline than Calhoun wanted to muster.

But he did it all the same – sidling out of the range of the warmth and moving in a wide arc out into the meadow. He wanted to come at Chatham from a direction the man wasn't expecting.

In the flickering light of the fire, Calhoun could see Chatham now. The man had rolled himself over onto his back, scooted around so that he was facing back into his camp, and drawn both his guns. He held them out in front of himself, high in the air, pointing back to the fire.

Calhoun dropped into a low squat and cautiously made his way deeper into the meadow, farther away from the light of the fire where he would be harder to see.

Henry Chatham reminded him of an injured elk, unable to stand and walk, eyes wide and frightened, shaking its heavy antlers in a desperate act to ward off danger.

"Show yourself Calhoun!" Chatham shouted into the campsite, still thinking that Moses was there.

Calhoun stayed quiet.

"You shot me good," Chatham shouted again. "But I ain't dead. So step on out here and let's finish this thing."

Without dropping his gun, Chatham pressed one hand into the snow beside him and tried to push himself up to his feet, but he fell back into the snow, cursing under his breath.

"I'm dying, Calhoun," Chatham called at the camp. "I can't move my dang legs. Come on out here and face me. Let's have an end to this."

From where he crouched in the snow, Calhoun had a clear and easy shot. They were a mite far for pistol shot, but Chatham wasn't moving.

Calhoun thumbed back the hammer of the gun, and when he did Chatham heard the noise.

Chatham rolled, throwing both guns up and shooting in the direction where he'd heard the cock of the hammer.

As fast as he could thumb back the hammers, Chatham fired again. And again.

Calhoun threw himself forward into the snow, burrowing himself deep so that he was as close to the ground as he could be. He threw his arms up over his head to protect him from being shot in the top of the head if one of Chatham's bullet should find him.

Henry Chatham was shooting wildly, blind to the target in the darkness. He'd been looking into the fire, and his eyes could see nothing in the pitch black farther out in the meadow where Calhoun hugged the earth.

Desperation drove Henry Chatham. He'd fired six wild shots, but accurate enough with all of them sailing just over Calhoun.

He drew back the hammers on both guns and fired again, still shooting blindly into the blackness.

And again.

For both men, the sudden explosion of gunfire had left their ears ringing. Calhoun had tried to count the shots, but he couldn't be sure. Eight? Maybe ten. Or was it just nine. Maybe Chatham had saved back one chamber on one gun.

Now Calhoun stretched his arm far off to his side, holding it up out of the snow, and he fired a shot that arced out over the empty valley meadow.

Henry Chatham let loose his last two shots directly at the muzzle flash. One ball grazed the cylinder of the Colt Navy, but Calhoun didn't care about the gun. He tossed it aside and threw his arm under him.

With the strength he had left, Moses Calhoun launched himself off the ground, pushing with his one good arm and springing from his feet.

Henry Chatham hadn't even done as good a job as Calhoun of counting rounds.

He was shot in the back and paralyzed in his legs. He was a dying and desperate man, and he's shot into the darkness not for survival but to be sure he took to the grave with him the man who'd sent him to the grave.

And now, with the big mountain hunter springing to life before him, Henry Chatham was all out of rounds. He'd shot off six chambers in two guns without hitting his target, and in the light of the fire he could now at last see Moses Calhoun coming at him, jerking free the hatchet he wore on his belt, raising that hatchet high over his head, and like a vision of the black-cloaked Grim Reaper himself, swinging the hatchet with the force of fury.

The hatchet cracked skull and brain, and then all was black and unknowing.

- 19 -

Moses Calhoun fell into the snow beside his vanquished foe, having spent every bit of energy he possessed.

All he wanted now was to sleep, though he knew he would be just as dead as Henry Chatham if he did not get up and move to the fire. His heavy coat and blankets, the warmth of the fire, nourishment – all he needed to keep himself alive was just over there in the orange glow.

The snow was so cold and froze him in all those places it touched – his face, his arms and wrists, under his shirt. He'd buried himself deep in the snow to avoid Chatham's shots, and now his entire torso the bandages wrapped around it wet with snow, seemed frozen in ice.

He stayed like this longer than he should have. Half-buried in the deep snow, the rush of blood and enthusiasm brought on by sudden action now fading, his body was beginning to shut down again in the cold. Calhoun thought of the buffalo cows that tunneled through the deep snow in the dead of winter, shaking their heavy heads, stomping down the thick layers of snow, all to get their calves to feeding grounds. Sometimes, when the work was finished, their bodies simply gave out and they fell dead.

Their calves would survive as part of the herd down in the valley near a river fed by heated waters from geysers and hot springs. That river always seemed to be on fire in the winter because of the steam coming up from the heated waters. The fish that thrived in the river attracted smaller animals – otters and beaver. The vegetation that pushed through the snows in the low valley, fed by the warmth from the river, also attracted mice and squirrels and bigger mammals like deer and bison. The red fox, coyotes, wolves, and the big cats all found prey among the smaller mammals.

The low valley with the smoking river teamed with life, even in the dead of winter, but the fight there for survival also meant death.

"We're no different," Calhoun said, speaking into the snow, talking to the corpse of his defeated enemy. He did not know if he said the words out loud or merely thought them in his head.

The cold seemed complete, all encompassing, and Calhoun's mind stayed with the buffalo cows that fell from exhaustion, never to get up again. He wondered if it was enough for them to know that their calves would survive.

He thought of Daniel and Elijah. They would be fine through the winter. There was meat enough, and plenty of wood. The cabin would keep them warm and their mother would see that they were fed. But how would they survive the next winter? Calhoun's job, as a father, was much harder than the buffalo cows. It wasn't enough to lead his children into a valley. He had to teach them to hunt. He had to teach them to track game, to skin a buffalo or a bear, to find the flowering plants and the shrubs and the trees that could heal wounds or ailments. There was so much he hadn't yet done to prepare them to survive.

His final conscious thoughts fell on Aka Ne'ai and her children, given to a Christian family in the town to raise them up in a way that was foreign to them, wrong for them. The ways of their father and grandfather would be forgotten to them.

Perhaps Aka Ne'ai could survive the winter with Chester Klemp. Chester was a decent man, and he would care for her if she could make it back to his cabin. And come spring, if she could get to the town, maybe they would give her children back to her. But Calhoun knew how the townspeople could be – always thinking they knew best, that their ways were best.

The cold wrapped around him like a blanket.

- 20 -

The warmth of the fire woke Moses Calhoun.

He heard the branches crackling and popping, felt the heat from the licking flames.

For a moment, Calhoun simply stayed where he was, feeling the warmth without understanding it. Even behind his closed eyelids, he could tell it was growing light outside, early dawn. His eyes came open with some difficulty, and through the bare branches of the aspens he could see gray clouds above him. His senses started to awaken, and Calhoun realized he had something beneath his head, a blanket or something soft. He was wrapped in a wool blanket, too. Somehow he was beside the fire, close enough to feel the heat from the flames. The fire had stayed alive through the night, though it was diminished from the large fire Henry Chatham had built.

Between the blanket and the fire, Calhoun felt truly warm.

It would have been easy for him to stay where he was, but he was lying on his injured back, and the ache of it made him roll so that he was facing the fire.

On the opposite side of the fire he saw the horses and mules, hitched to a line running between two aspen trees. Among them was the bay gelding he'd ridden the day before in pursuit of Henry Chatham, the one he'd left tied deeper in the forest.

Someone had come and found him in the snow, pulled him to the fire and wrapped him in a blanket or two, and had also brought the bay over to the other horses and unsaddled it.

Calhoun's first thought was of Chester Klemp, thinking that somehow Aka Ne'ai had gotten to him and Chester had come through the night and found Calhoun before he succumbed to the cold. But that was impossible. There was no way that that Aka Ne'ai could have gotten to Chester so quickly, no way that Chester could have made the journey so fast.

The packed gear was on the ground not far from where the animals were tied, and Calhoun now saw movement near the packs. He squinted hard to see past the flames and smoke from the fire, and he saw an Indian kneeling at the gear, going through the packs.

Calhoun had friends among the Snake People – at

least, he did have before the soldiers attacked the winter camp the previous year. Since then, over the spring and summer, he'd seen only a few People from the tribe – refugees who had escaped the slaughter but were now adrift and alone in the valleys. Unlikely as it seemed, it was possible that some among the People who were still friendly toward him had wandered upon him in the night.

But then the Indian stood up, and Calhoun realized it was Eli Simmons' daughter, Aka Ne'ai.

"Where'd you come from?" Calhoun asked, and his voice came out like a hoarse croak.

Aka Ne'ai started, not realizing he was awake.

She looked at him across the fire, through the gray smoke.

"You're alive?" she asked, a note of surprise in her voice.

"I am," Calhoun said. "And I suppose it's thanks to you."

Aka Ne'ai nodded.

"I found you in the snow," she said.

With some difficulty, Calhoun pushed himself up to a seated position, and the blankets started to fall away. He realized then that he was no longer wearing his shirt, and the bandages around his chest were also gone. His feet were likewise naked. He only had on his britches. He saw that Aka Ne'ai had put a blanket beneath him and covered him in a couple of wool blankets from the packs. She's topped the blankets with his heavy bearskin coat. Calhoun now slid himself into the coat, finding the effort to be exhausting.

"I fed you some pine tea while you slept," Aka Ne'ai

said. "But I was not sure you would awaken."

His limbs were stiff and sore. A burning sensation under his arms told him that Aka Ne'ai had tied him to a horse to drag him to the fire. She'd done well to keep him alive.

The pain and rumbling in his stomach was a good sign – he was hungry. His body wanted to regain its strength. He started to push himself to his feet, thinking to make himself some breakfast, but his arm was too weak and his legs did not care to move.

Calhoun understood more than he remembered. Aka Ne'ai had stripped him of his clothes. Probably she had vigorously rubbed the life back into his limbs, his fingers and his toes. And she had taken off her own clothes, or some portion of them, and laid with him under the blanket. The warmth of their naked flesh, side-by-side, had kept him alive.

"You should lie back down," Aka Ne'ai said. "I will make some breakfast, and then I need to wrap fresh bandages on your wound."

Calhoun nodded. He pulled the blankets back over him and fell back onto the blanket.

He watched Aka Ne'ai. She'd gathered up the food that Henry Chatham had tossed into the air during the fight the night before, and now she set about cooking what they had.

Calhoun twisted to look out into the meadow. He could see Chatham's body. The cleaved head was a mess. Calhoun turned back away from it. He derived no joy from taking the man's life, but there was satisfaction in surviving.

"You decided not to go to Chester's cabin?" Calhoun

asked.

"I decided I had to get to town to be with my children," Aka Ne'ai said.

She had walked all day, following along in the trail made by Chatham's caravan of animals. Calhoun thought of the buffalo cows tunneling through the snow.

"I'm obliged to you," he said. "You've saved my life twice."

Aka Ne'ai nodded at him.

"Had it not been for you keeping a promise to my father, I probably would have died at the winter camp when the soldiers attacked," Aka Ne'ai said. "We do what we can for those who do for us."

***

The snow had stopped falling, though the sky above remained gray with low, rolling clouds that looked as if they might start loosing snow again at any moment.

Calhoun decided to leave the bodies. The four outlaws and the bounty Henry Chatham sought, meant nothing to him. They'd paid the debt they owed for killing Eli Simmons, and the wolves could have them now. Any money their bodies might fetch in Denver or anywhere else didn't matter to Moses Calhoun. He'd not come after them for the money, and he would not take it now. Chatham, too, meant nothing to him. If the man had believed him when Calhoun said that he didn't care about the money, he'd be alive now.

The winters were harsh, and it seemed a waste to take these bodies to the town where they would go to waste in a grave. The wolves and coyotes and would appreciate the meals.

The one concession to decency that Calhoun made, though, was to tie Paul Bentsen's body to a mule and drag the body a ways into the woods. In a ravine, Calhoun found some loose rocks, and he piled the rocks on top of the body, making the best grave he could. There were not enough rocks to sufficiently cover the body, and Calhoun lacked the strength to try to dig even a little bit into the ground. Wolves would get to him, but probably Calhoun had buried him well enough that there would be something left if his family tried to find him.

Calhoun did not wait long after eating before he began packing the gear. He was weak, and his left arm was all but useless, and Aka Ne'ai had to help him to lift the panniers and the saddles, but by the time he stepped into the sorrel's stirrup and hefted himself into the saddle, Calhoun was feeling stronger. He'd eaten a feast of smoked sausage and biscuits, the best of what Aka Ne'ai could find in the provisions. She'd made coffee, and boiled more pine tea. Calhoun was not wholly restored, perhaps, but warm inside and feeling more alive than he had since the previous morning when Henry Chatham shot him in the back.

The last thing, before stepping into the saddle, Calhoun reloaded the chambers of the Colt Navy and replaced all the percussion caps. Whatever else they might face on what remained of their journey through the valley wasn't likely to be more than a pack of wolves or a big cat, but Calhoun knew that he'd be hard-pressed to fend off anything bigger than a red fox with his hatchet. He was too stiff, too sore, and too exhausted to put up much of a fight. But if he had to, he could still squeeze a trigger.

And so they made their own caravan, Moses Calhoun and Aka Ne'ai, leading the horses and mules of dead men, riding out through the meadow.

Sore and aching from his neck to his ankles, Calhoun felt at least a little restored now. Though he often left his bearskin coat in his pannier when he rode, even in the cold, today he wore it, relishing in the warmth that had eluded him all the day before. He would have liked to feel the sun on his face, but the clouds persisted in the sky.

"It's a mite warmer today, maybe," Calhoun said to Aka Ne'ai.

"You're warmer because you have your coat," she said.

"That may be it," Calhoun said, offering her a grin.

They rode side by side now, or near enough to it. Calhoun was back mounted on his sorrel – a horse that knew him better than he knew himself. Hurting and tired, though he was, being on the horse felt as comfortable to him as being in his own cabin. Aka Ne'ai was on the bay gelding again, and the bay had a habit of wanting to be up in the lead. He seemed satisfied to share the lead with the sorrel, but he did not want to be behind. So they rode side-by-side, or near enough to it, trailing the other horses and mules.

Calhoun could not be sure if it was a dream or a snatch of memory or a vision imagined, but he had in his mind a picture of Eli Simmons' daughter lying beside him under the blankets, both of them unclothed, as she tried to use her heat to keep him alive. The ache under his arms gave him some sense of the lengths she'd gone to while he was unconscious in order to get him near the fire.

"I'm obliged to you for what you did for me last night," he told her. "I expect I'd have woke up dead if you'd not come along."

Aka Ne'ai gave a small smile and lowered her eyes.

On long hunts, Calhoun could spend days alone in the forests and valley meadows without uttering a word, unless it was a command to a stubborn mule or an exclamation at a good shot. Conversation among men like Calhoun was not over-valued. But for a reason he could not understand, he felt now that he needed to make some talk with the woman.

"I'm sorry your husband never came for you after the soldiers attacked the winter camp last year," Calhoun said.

Aka Ne'ai nodded her head without much emotion showing on her face.

"It's the way of things," she said. "Men fight and kill each other; women raise their sons to fight and kill."

"Will you stay in the town?" Calhoun asked.

Aka Ne'ai shrugged her shoulders.

"It's not like here where you store up for the winter," she said. "In the town, you have to have money to get food. We have no money."

Calhoun twisted in the saddle, though it hurt him to do so, and he reached into one of his saddlebags where he had stashed Eli Simmons' money purse, the one he'd taken off Harlan Mullen.

"This was your father's money," Calhoun said, holding the leather sack out where Aka Ne'ai could reach for it. "You take this. There's money enough to see you through the winter there."

Whatever life Aka Ne'ai might be able to put together for herself and her children down in the town once that money ran out was likely to be a hard one. A half-breed Indian woman with two small children didn't have much hope in a white man's town, and Calhoun did not envy the future she would have to carve out for herself. She'd be better off with the Snake People. As the widow of a chief's son, they would be more apt look after her. Of course, the Snake People were half-starved even before the white soldiers attacked their winter camp and massacred so many of them. It might be that her husband's people were no better off than she would be in the town. If he didn't already have a wife, Calhoun knew he would have taken her in. She was a fine looking woman, and she'd proven herself resourceful. In these mountains, a resourceful woman carried a lot of value as a wife.

"Maybe in the spring you should take your boys and visit Chester Klemp," Calhoun suggested.

Aka Ne'ai glanced at him and then shook her head.

"Are you going to fix everything for me, Moses Calhoun?" she asked. Her tone had an angry bite to it. "Are you going to send me up to the mountains to be the wife of a hunter that only wants to read books? He can replace my husband and my father and provide for me and my children?"

Calhoun gave a shrug.

"You could do worse than Chester," he said, feeling a mite admonished.

Aka Ne'ai grunted a scoff at him.

"I can look after myself and my sons," she said.

Calhoun chuckled.

"I reckon you can," he said.

- 21 -

If Calhoun had hoped to make it through the valley in three days, he soon discovered that he had been too optimistic.

Including the day he spent tracking Henry Chatham, it looked like it was going to be four full days and part of a fifth.

Calhoun's injuries were such that he had to rely on Aka Ne'ai more than he would have liked. She collected wood for fires. She cooked the meals, though they were down to just jerky and hardtack now, and the meals were

PEECHER

little more than sustenance. The smoked meat had a
decent taste to it, and they fried it in a pan and then put
the hardtack down in the little bit of grease that cooked
from the jerky, but they offered only a little in terms of
flavor and nothing in variety. But sustenance was all that
mattered. Surviving the trek through the valley was all
that mattered.

But they had little reason to worry.

They had provisions enough, such as they were. Both
Aka Ne'ai and Moses Calhoun had coats and blankets to
keep them warm. There was little, if any, chance that they
would encounter danger in the valley now. The snow was
piled fairly deep, and the only people they might see at
this point would be friends, local trappers who knew
Calhoun and were running their traps along one of the
creeks running down into the valley. But it seemed
unlikely that they would even encounter anyone like that.
The trappers would have pulled in all but a few traps
now, and those would be the ones closest to their own
cabins. Calhoun also doubted that they would have to
worry about attack from animals. Maybe a pack of wolves
or a big cat, but he didn't think so. With so many horses
and mules, and two people, they did not make an easy
prey. Only a grizzly bear might think of rushing in and
trying to take a horse or a mule, and the bear had surely
gone in for the winter.

Despite his injuries, Calhoun saw no reason now to
worry that he wouldn't make it home.

He'd not taken a fever. Aka Ne'ai had cleaned the
wound on his back and doctored him such that it seemed
unlikely he would infect. The tea she had given him
helped some with the pain, though a dull ache persisted
in his hip, and his back felt like it was being slit open with
a hot knife.

Still, Calhoun knew that injuries heal and pain disperses in the memory.

With no fresh snow falling, the packed snow in the valley meadow took on a hard appearance, like the horses should be walking on top of it instead of crunching through it with each footfall. The rhythmic crunching of the horses, the soft, cool breeze, all made Calhoun desperate to doze off to sleep. And in the saddle, he did doze some. Though his cheeks felt the prickly sting of the cold air, he was warm inside the bearskin coat, and his heavy eyelids kept drooping. He would submit to them at times, allowing his head to loll on his shoulders, but he would come back awake with a quick start.

Aka Ne'ai did not talk. She allowed him this jittery rest, knowing that too much exertion could delay his ability to heal.

One of the times he jerked up with a start, Calhoun's eyes fell immediately on some whirl of orange against the white backdrop of the valley, a movement up ahead, a blur of color.

He leaned forward in his saddle some and squinted at it.

There it was again – a quick pop, and a fall, out on the side of a small rise.

"Red fox," Calhoun said.

"He's looking for mice," Aka Ne'ai agreed.

Calhoun gave a slight push with his knee to turn the sorrel wide of the fox, toward the other side of the meadow. No sense chasing him away from his work.

As they neared, the fox gave them a curious stare, and then he went back to what he was doing.

They watched as the fox sprang up into the air and then came down with all its weight on its front paws, caving in the small burrow of a field mice. The fox stuffed his head inside, his hind legs digging at the snow as he tried to get purchase to push himself deeper into the mouse's burrow. And then he came out, a little prance in his step. They could just make out the black spot in his mouth.

"He'll make it a week on that prize," Calhoun said.

They'd shifted their position in the meadow by fifty or sixty yards, riding nearer now to the tree line at their left, and paying attention to the fox the way they had been, Calhoun did not immediately notice the holes in the snow. But now he did. Spaced a perfect distance apart, filled in some with fresh snow.

"Horse tracks," Aka Ne'ai said, also noticing the long line of holes pressed into the snow that stretched as far toward the horizon as they could see.

Calhoun nodded.

"Bearclaw Jim," he said.

"The guide who was with those men who killed my father?" Aka Ne'ai said.

"That's the one," Moses Calhoun said.

They continued on some distance, following in the tracks. Moses Calhoun remained quiet, thoughtful.

He'd made an enemy of Bearclaw Jim a year ago when he'd shot the man's finger and thumb off, and the old army scout had not forgotten Moses Calhoun.

If he was smart, Jim had ridden on into town, but a man with a grudge can often engage in dumb behavior.

The tracks in the snow were at least a day old

because snow had fallen in them and covered them up. Traveling alone, Bearclaw Jim had made good time through the valley. So long as those tracks were not fresh, Calhoun did not have to worry. So far as Bearclaw Jim knew, Calhoun would be traveling with Henry Chatham, bringing back prisoners. He did not know how it all settled out with Harlan Mullen's gang, and he certainly did not know that Henry Chatham had betrayed Calhoun. He had no reason to believe that Moses Calhoun, a man he hated, was riding injured and alone with a squaw.

The afternoon wore on, and Moses Calhoun found himself thoroughly exhausted when at last he pointed to a cliff face up ahead on the mountain beside them.

"We should make camp there," he said.

"It's early in the afternoon," Aka Ne'ai said, and Calhoun realized how determined the woman was to reach town and get to her children.

"If we go on much farther, we'll be making camp in the dark," Calhoun said. "Besides, I happen to know that below that cliff face is a good overhang. We'll have a dry camp, sheltered from the wind. A few spruce boughs and we can fix it up tight as a cabin."

Aka Ne'ai frowned. She could live with a wet and drafty camp if it meant going on, getting closer to town, but Calhoun was insistent and she knew the man felt weak and tired. So at last she relented, and Calhoun maneuvered the sorrel horse toward a trail that cut deep through the spruce trees and took them directly down to the cliff face.

With a glance, Aka Ne'ai saw that this place was superior for camping. The cliff face widened and jutted out toward the bottom, and then it opened up in a big arc, a shallow cave large enough for Calhoun to stand in the center of it.

Calhoun tied the horses near to the cave. Here under the spruce trees and the cliff face, the snow fell irregularly, and there were plenty of spots where the horses could pick through the snow to find forage.

Aka Ne'ai helped him drag their gear in under the rock shelter.

In several places there were remnants of campfires on the stone and dirt floor of the shallow cave, evidence that this place was well known as a shelter.

"You have slept here before?" Aka Ne'ai asked.

"Many times," Calhoun said. "On long hunts I've used this cave more times than I can count."

She had to admit that it was a cozy place, though the stone floor and ceiling held the cold and seemed to push it into the space between.

Aka Ne'ai used Calhoun's Bowie knife to cut spruce branches and weaved them together to create a wall that would cover some of the cave entrance and help to block some of the breeze.

At the mouth of the cave she made a fire with Calhoun helping her. He did not object when she built the fire up fairly large, though in the back of his mind he thought of cats and wolves and the danger the fire might mean for the animals. But all told, they had a dozen animals, horses and mules, and Calhoun thought it unlikely that a cat would try to get a horse from such a large pack.

Aka Ne'ai heated up jerky and hardtack for them.

"I'll be glad to get home and have a stew," Calhoun said. "Something with a little taste to it."

"I just want to get home and get my sons," Aka Ne'ai said. "I'd eat jerky and biscuits forever if I can get them back."

He understood her worry. Sometimes white folks, in the name of Christian duty, did some foolish things. He could see where people in the town might object to turning the two boys over to their savage mother.

"We'll get them back," Calhoun said.

Calhoun did not sleep well through the night. The rock-hard floor of the cave discovered new ways to make his injuries jab at him, and when he woke before dawn with the fire burned out and the cold penetrating the cave despite their wall of woven spruce branches, Calhoun felt stiff and uncomfortable.

Another day in the saddle was going to leave his injured hip all seized up.

***

On the fifth day out, around mid-morning, Calhoun and Aka Ne'ai reached a place where the valley turned to the northeast and where the forest opened and, looking from a rise, Calhoun could at last see the farm that Ethan Corder called home.

The previous afternoon they had passed by the trail leading up to Moses Calhoun's cabin. With the snow making the trail dangerous, they would have been at least two hours getting up to his cabin, but they could have stayed the night there. Calhoun considered it without mentioning his cabin to Aka Ne'ai, and in the end decided against it.

Kee Kuttai would have mutinied against his leaving the cabin to take Aka Ne'ai to town, especially when she saw the condition he was in. And, in truth, he would have found it hard to take that first step out of the cabin door.

So they rode on, camping one last night in the valley before coming to Ethan Corder's farm in the early afternoon. They found Corder in his barn, mucking the horse stalls.

"Mose," Corder said, a genuine concern on his face when he saw the state of the man. "What in hell happened to you?"

"That bounty hunter you brought to me shot me in the back," Corder said. "We rounded up Harlan Mullen and them other two, but as we started to make our way back, I guess Mr. Chatham decided he did not want to split the bounty money with me."

Corder immediately went to work helping Calhoun and Aka Ne'ai with the horses and mules. They unburdened them and brushed them down, and Corder moved them into a paddock and got fresh straw for them. While they did the work, Moses Calhoun told Corder about the encounter with Mullen's gang at Chester Klemp's cabin. He told Ethan Corder about Chatham's betrayal, and how Calhoun followed him to get back his property.

"I left the bodies – Mullen's gang, that boy Bentsen, and Chatham – all at the campsite where I caught him," Calhoun said. "I reckon an enterprising man who wants to earn the bounty could still go up there and get whatever the wolves haven't taken."

With the animals dealt with and in the paddock, they moved from the barn to Corder's house where his wife dished them up some supper. One thing Moses Calhoun always appreciated about Ethan Corder was that no one left his home hungry. Strangers and friends alike could always pass Corder's farm and find a meal for free.

Corder turned up his nose.

"I ain't that kind of enterprising," he said. "But once word spreads through town that those bodies are back up there, I reckon someone will go for them."

"I felt some remorse about leaving Bentsen like that," Calhoun said. "He never did me a wrong."

"What will you do now?"

"I'm taking Aka Ne'ai back to town," Calhoun said. "I want to see to it that she gets her children back."

Corder pursed his lips and made a grunt. He understood as well as Calhoun that the folks in town might be disinclined to return the woman's children to her.

"We'll go in the morning," Corder said, sparing a glance to the Indian woman who had remained silent. "I'll ride with you. We'll go together to talk to Sheriff Wooten."

Calhoun swallowed a bite of food and took a drink of the hot tea Corder's wife had poured for him.

"I reckon I can talk to him on my own," Calhoun said. "One way or another, I expect I can bring him to see reason."

Ethan Corder laughed.

"That's why I think I should go with you," he said. "I feel some responsibility in all this. I brought those men to you, got you involved in it. I'd hate to see you spend the winter in the town's jail."

"Small chance of that," Calhoun said darkly.

Ethan Corder dropped the conversation. He'd sensed Moses Calhoun's mood and didn't see any need to prod him further.

Corder lived an existence between the folks in town and the trappers and hunters who lived in the isolation of the mountains. He knew that as much as the townspeople might mean well with the things they did, their rules and interference could irk a mountain man into violence. Men like Moses Calhoun did not readily accept well-intentioned meddling.

"I have one other question for you," Calhoun said after eating a bit more.

"What's that?"

"Day before yesterday we started following some tracks in the snow," Calhoun said. "We followed them all the way up to your barn."

Corder nodded.

"That old scout – Bearclaw Somebody – he rode in yesterday around midday. He said he'd witnessed some of the battle between Chatham and those men y'all went to fetch. Said Chatham let him through because he had no part in any of it."

Calhoun nodded.

"All true," he said.

"Told me he didn't hang around long enough to see the outcome."

"Also true," Calhoun said.

"I fed him, and then he kept on, trying to make town before nightfall."

Calhoun nodded again, satisfied that Bearclaw Jim was not lying in wait, planning an ambush. His other concern, though mild, was that Bearclaw Jim might wander up to Calhoun's cabin and find Kee Kuttai and the boys alone and unprotected. Not that Kee Kuttai wouldn't put a load of buckshot in Bearclaw Jim's gut, but all the same, Calhoun worried about his family.

After they ate, Ethan Corder made up pallets of blankets for his children and gave Calhoun and Aka Ne'ai beds to sleep in. He also gave Calhoun a salve for his injured back, and fresh bandages. Aka Ne'ai, who had doctored him so far, removed the bloody and frozen bandages, and then she applied the slave and fresh bandages.

"You'll recover fine," she said. "It's already beginning to heal."

Those were almost the only words she bothered to speak the entire time they were at Ethan Corder's farm, though she did thank Corder's wife for the food and the bed.

She was an odd woman, having come up early in her life with old Eli Simmons and then being raised into adulthood with the Snake People. Calhoun was not sure if she remained silent because she was uncomfortable in front of Corder and his wife, or if it was because she did not trust them.

- 22 -

Sheriff Wooten's office was just a small log cabin with a chair and a desk and a bench where Calhoun sat while he told the sheriff of what had transpired in the valley. Aka Ne'ai sat beside Calhoun, and Ethan Corder stood against the wall by the door.

Calhoun left Chester Klemp's name out of it, simply referring to him as a man who lives in a cabin up on the far mountain range. He told the sheriff about the shooting at the cabin

"I can make a map to Paul Bentsen's body, if that's

something his family would want," Calhoun said.

Sheriff Wooten nodded, looking grave. "Probably should. They wouldn't go until spring, but I reckon they'll want to give him a decent burial."

Calhoun grunted.

"Might not be much left to bury," he said.

Wooten raised his eyebrows.

"I'll find a way to tell them so," the sheriff said.

He took a heavy breath, examining Moses Calhoun in the dim light cast by the lantern. The man showed in every way the difficulty of his journey, and Sheriff Wooten felt more than a little regret at having been the catalyst to drag Calhoun into this.

"You know, Mr. Calhoun, I'd have never brought that man Chatham to you if I'd known he would try a trick like that," Wooten said. He despised a killer, but a back-shooting coward was the worst of all.

"I don't hold you to account for any of it," Calhoun said.

Calhoun, Aka Ne'ai, and Ethan Corder rode through the day and arrived in the town around dusk. They found Sheriff Wooten just leaving his office to go home for supper.

"I suppose that bounty on the three of them will go to you now," Sheriff Wooten said. "The sheriff in Denver might be reluctant to pay without having evidence that Mullen and the others are dead, but I'll vouch for you."

"I ain't interested in the bounty," Calhoun said. "I got the one thing I went after. But we have a matter we need to work out."

Sheriff Wooten narrowed his eyes and gave a glance at Aka Ne'ai. From the moment she'd taken a seat on the sheriff's bench, the woman's jaw was set in a look of defiance, and the sheriff had already surmised what was coming next.

Wooten shifted in his seat.

"I'll tell you, the feeling in town is that those two boys are better off with a Christian family."

Calhoun stood up and reached his hand to his belt where he had slung his hatchet with the beaded leather handle.

"That Christian family won't do those boys a damn bit of good if I have to go and take back Aka Ne'ai's children," Calhoun said. "I'll not trifle with this, Sheriff Wooten. She'll have her children back, one way or another."

Exhausted from the ride to town, the man didn't hardly have the strength to stand, but Sheriff Wooten did not doubt his sincerity.

Ethan Corder stepped away from the wall and put a calming hand on Calhoun's shoulder.

"Why don't you and the woman step outside," Corder said.

Calhoun's eyes flashed dangerously as he turned his glare from the sheriff to Corder. But Calhoun knew Corder to be a friend, and he softened a bit and nodded. Calhoun glanced back at Aka Ne'ai, and the two of them walked together out into the cold dusk.

Moses Calhoun made one or two trips into the town every year. He could remember when the town wasn't much more than the old trading post where he still went to sell his pelts. Anymore, mostly he just traded pelts for supplies – he found no use for money up in the mountains. But sometimes he'd take a handful of coins because the boys liked to play with them, especially the shiny ones. Now the town was quite a bit more than it once was. Houses and a couple of taverns, a half dozen stores. Most of them were all general stores, selling everything from shoes and shot to blankets and seed. There were a couple of lawyers in town, and a doctor, and two butchers, and around the town there were a couple dozen small farms like Ethan Corder's. Up on a hill just on the outskirts of town, a church with a squat steeple loomed over everything.

Even now, at dusk, there were so many people going about that the tiny town seemed like a metropolis.

From the sheriff's office, Calhoun could hear angry voices being raised.

"Their mother is alive, and it ain't right not to give them over to her," Ethan Corder said, his voice raised so loud that his words were audible through the glass window.

Now there was continued grumbling between them.

Aka Ne'ai gave Calhoun a worried glance.

"You'll have your children back," Calhoun said.

He leaned back against the door frame, and with the toe of his boot he pushed open the door just a touch, so that he could hear what the two men said.

"Look, Ethan, it's not that I even disagree with you," Sheriff Wooten said. "But you know how folks can get. They get it in their heads that them boys need to be raised up by white folks, and next thing you know, the whole town is in favor of it."

"Mike, we've been friends since I come up to this valley to set down roots," Corder said. "And that man out there, he's been my friend just as long. I probably know him better than anyone else in this town does. And I can guarantee you this – if you don't give those children over to their mother, Moses Calhoun is going to set this town on fire and burn out everyone he don't kill. That Mullen gang was a dangerous outfit. And that bounty hunter wasn't no slouch, neither. And you see standing out there the man that came out of all that alive. The rest of 'em are all dead. Is that the man you want to make enemies with?"

Sheriff Wooten sighed heavily.

"Wait here with them," he said. "I'll go and fetch the boys."

Without a word, Sheriff Wooten stepped past Calhoun and Aka Ne'ai, and he walked down through the town a couple of blocks and then turned down a side street. Ethan Corder came outside and watched him walk away.

When the sheriff was out of sight, Corder said, "I told him you'd lay waste to the town if he didn't give the woman her children."

Calhoun nodded.

"You told him right."

***

Later, when the children were returned to Aka Ne'ai, Calhoun and Corder went with her back to Eli Simmons' cabin.

His old friend's blood was still on the slat boards that made up the floor of the cabin. Eli's old Lancaster rifle hung above the mantle on the rock chimney.

Ethan Corder made up a fire in the fireplace. Aka Ne'ai made a stew of the vegetables that were still in the pantry.

But Moses Calhoun fell asleep on a cot without eating.

- 23 -

Ethan Corder's farm was just about a day's ride from town, and another day's ride would put Calhoun back home.

He'd gone too hard, for too long, and he felt now that he was beginning to shut down. Exhaustion seemed to press down on him like an invisible weight across his shoulders.

The two men were only an hour out of town, returning to Corder's farm, but Ethan Corder could see Moses Calhoun slumped in his saddle, looking weak.

"You should rest a day or two at my farm," Corder said.

Calhoun nodded and gave a grunt.

"Probably," he said. "But I'm ready to be home. I miss my wife and my boys."

"Be better to rest a couple of days, get your strength, and still be alive when you see them," Corder said, offering an ironic chuckle.

Calhoun did not respond, and the two men rode some distance with Calhoun dozing in his saddle. He woke with a start when he felt Ethan Corder ride along next to him and prop him back up.

"Damn near slid out of the saddle, Mose," Corder said. "I wish you'd think about staying a couple of days with me. Let us take care of you, get some decent food in you, and then you go on home."

Moses Calhoun shook his head awake and sat up a bit straighter in his saddle.

"I'll accept your hospitality for the night tonight, and in the morning, I'll be fit as a fiddle," he said. "At least enough to get home."

Ethan Corder shook his head and pursed his lips in a disapproving way, but he knew it was pointless to argue with the man.

Moses Calhoun and Chester Klemp and Eli Simmons and all those other men who chose to live in the mountains, removed from all society, did not make it on their own up there like that because they lacked for stubbornness, and Ethan Corder knew better than to waste his time trying to persuade a man like Moses Calhoun when his mind was set.

And so they continued on through the day, Moses half sleeping in his saddle. They came to Ethan Corder's farm in the valley about an hour before dusk, and Corder had one of his sons tend to the horses in the barn. He had to help Calhoun into the farmhouse and laid him down on a cot near the fireplace where Moses fell fast asleep. After a couple of hours, Ethan Corder's wife went to the man with a bowl of stew and Calhoun was able to wake up enough to eat some.

Worried that he was catching a fever and that the wound on his back had turned, Corder and his wife got Moses up enough to change and redress the wound. There was no smell to it, nor did it give an appearance of infection.

"Poor man is just exhausted," Corder's wife observed.

Corder nodded agreement.

"I reckon he'll spend the winter hibernating like an old grizzly."

In the morning, Calhoun woke to the sound of voices and not knowing where he was. It took his mind a long time to clear the fog and remember that he was at Ethan Corder's farm, and it took some time after that to remember that he had a long ride ahead of him.

He rose and found himself shirtless with fresh bandages. His boots were beside the fire with his socks laid over them.

Ethan Corder had constructed a large house with two bedrooms, a living room and a parlor, and a kitchen and dining room. Corder and his wife and at least some of their children, were already eating breakfast when Moses Calhoun left his cot in the living room and found them at the supper table.

"Morning, Mose," Ethan Corder said. "I wasn't going to let you sleep much longer. I assume you're still determined to make for home today?"

Calhoun nodded. He felt a mite better, though not much.

"I wish you'd reconsider, Mr. Calhoun," Ethan's wife said.

"Ma'am, I'm grateful to you for what you've done for me," Moses said. "But I'm about as ready as a man can be to get home to my wife and sons. I imagine I'll perk right up when I get home."

They had ham and eggs and toasted bread for breakfast, and Moses ate what he could with them. Weak as he was, he knew he needed to eat, but he just didn't have much appetite.

And then he was at the barn, Ethan Corder helping him into the saddle.

"You'll have a good day for travel," Corder said, looking back at the sun rising in the eastern sky. "Sun's coming up, not a cloud. Day might even warm up a bit for you."

"I appreciate all you and your family have done for me, and especially your help with the sheriff," Calhoun said.

"I'm glad to do it for you, Mose," Corder said. "You just take care that you don't doze off and fall out of that saddle. And when you get home, you rest up good."

Corder watched him with some worry as Calhoun rode away, still slumped and looking weak and small atop his horse.

What neither man saw was the stirring in the forest beyond Ethan Corder's farm. A man with a bad hand and an undying grudge also watched Moses Calhoun riding away.

And like Ethan Corder, Bearclaw Jim saw that Moses Calhoun was in a weakened state.

***

Bearclaw Jim walked a ways through the forest, leading his horse. He wanted to avoid being seen.

Moses Calhoun rode past him, out in the wide-open valley he was easy enough for Jim to keep an eye on.

There was a time when Bearclaw Jim would have simply watched Calhoun down the barrel of a long gun and when he was sure of his target, he'd have put the man on the ground from eighty yards away. But Moses Calhoun had shot those days away from Bearclaw Jim when he sent a lead ball into the man's hand that swiped off his thumb and forefinger. Jim had practiced learning to shoot a rifle again, but he never could hold it steady enough to hit a target at any distance. He was a right-handed man, and his left hand had only ever been good in a supporting role to his right. He'd found it awkward to even learn how to use a fork with his left hand. He'd tried shooting with his left hand and found that to be a wasted effort. Even understanding how to hold the rifle and aim with his left eye had been confounding to him. He'd tried steadying the gun with his left hand and pulling the trigger with the right middle finger. That went a little better, but not much. With no thumb on his right hand to grip the rifle, he had no way of controlling the recoil of the gun, and he looked a fool with the gun bouncing around on his shoulder.

So shooting Moses Calhoun out of his saddle, as much as the thought appealed to him just now, was out of the question.

But the man was clearly weak. Whatever had happened up in the mountains had left Calhoun exhausted and broken, and Bearclaw Jim, seeing his opportunity, intended to make good on his grudge.

So he followed Calhoun, at first leading his horse through the woods and then finally coming out of the woods and mounting, riding along behind Calhoun at some distance.

The sorrel horse seemed to sense Calhoun's weakened state, and his gait was nothing more than a meander up through the valley.

As he rode behind, Bearclaw Jim thought he several times saw Calhoun start to slip from the saddle. He considered sliding his heavy Bowie knife from its scabbard and simply riding the man down, knocking him from the saddle and plunging the knife into his gut. He imagined the act over and over, a dozen times killing Calhoun in his mind. But as he continued to follow the man, Jim had to wonder if he would even get the chance. From a distance, the way Moses Calhoun sat in his saddle, it looked to Bearclaw Jim like any moment he might drop from the horse.

- 24 -

The bright sun shone in the afternoon sky like a small blessing, and when the sorrel horse left the valley and started up the trail toward home, Calhoun had a moment of regret to leave the warmth in the valley. But home was up on the side of the mountain, and the only way to get there was through the shade of the tall trees.

The horse knew its way home. Calhoun never had to touch a leg to the horse or drag a rein. And that was fine, because he did not have strength to do either.

As they climbed the long trail up the mountain,

Calhoun found himself nodding off again, as he'd been doing all day. His energy sapped, Calhoun struggled just to sit upright. But the horse knew the its way home and stuck to the unmarked trail, walking through draws and over a ridge. There were two good approaches to the cabin, neither of them marked trails. One came out in an open meadow with the house sitting at the far side. The other came up through the woods, along a draw and through a thick stand of fir trees that hid the house from view. The horse preferred the trail that came up through the fir trees as the shorter of the two routes, and it made now for the firs, quickening its step as the firs came into view. But Moses Calhoun did not see them. He knew they were near the cabin because he could hear the old yellow cur dog barking in the distance, always good to warn of visitors.

Calhoun's eyes were shut and his chin was in his chest when he heard the galloping behind him. In his half-awake state, Calhoun thought it must be Ethan Corder.

He started to twist in his saddle, though his back had stiffened up around the injury, and turning in the saddle to look behind him took a massive effort.

Calhoun knew the rider was nearly up to him now, and he'd still not worked his way around to face whoever it was.

And then a tremendous blow caught him in the side of the head as the rushing rider came even with him, the two horses colliding.

The sorrel gelding spooked and leapt forward.

Calhoun, his head whipping violently with the blow, lost his seating and fell violently from the horse.

His head spun, and he just had the presence of mind to jerk his foot free of the stirrup as the sorrel bolted on ahead without him. He'd fallen on his back, and the electric shock of pain sweeping through his mind interrupted the drowsiness.

Calhoun rolled off the path, sensing that he had to get clear of the horse and rider that were turning around ahead of him and starting back at him.

He rolled a couple of times until he came up against a large rock, and then he pushed with his one good hand to get himself up on his knees. He tried to look around for the man who'd attacked him, but blood was pouring from a gash in his head and he could not see a thing.

He heard the heavy landing of a man jumping from a horse, and then he felt a boot smash against his ribs.

Calhoun fell again, squeezing his ribs with his good arm.

"You're done in," a voice called at him, followed by cackling laughter. "You've had it, Calhoun."

Moses Calhoun coughed. With his left arm still bound in a sling he had to roll again to try to get his right arm under him. But he lacked the strength to push himself up. His face fell down in a pile of snow. He couldn't push himself off the ground, nor could he pick up his face. He didn't so much recognize the voice as he did intuitively know who it was. Bearclaw Jim had followed him from town, and while Calhoun slept in Ethan Corder's home, Jim had waited for him.

"Where's that old sorrel horse going?" Bearclaw Jim asked. "They say in town you've got a wife back at your cabin. Think that old horse is going to lead me back to your cabin?"

A boot smashed into the back of Calhoun's head, driving his face against the ground, and whatever consciousness he had left began to slip away from him.

"I could gut you like a hog now, and there ain't a thing you can do about it," Bearclaw Jim said. "You're useless. You just go on and die now, Calhoun. And know that while you're dying, I'm going to be paying a visit to your squaw."

The sorrel horse pushed its way through the fir trees and was then in sight of the cabin and the yellow dog barking from the front porch.

Bearclaw Jim knelt down now, pressing a knee against Calhoun's wounded back.

"Nothing left in you, not even to yelp, is there?" Jim said. "One last thing I've got to do, Moses Calhoun. You took from me my finger and thumb. Shot them right the hell off, didn't you?"

Jim pressed the flat blade of his knife against Calhoun's face.

"You feel that? You know what that is? That there's the knife that's going to take your finger and thumb, so when you die here on this trail, you'll know what it's like to be maimed for what's left of your life."

He took Calhoun's wrist in his grip and pulled the man's arm out from his body, pressing his weight to hold Calhoun's hand against the ground.

Calhoun did not have the strength to resist, but he balled his hand into a fist so that Bearclaw Jim couldn't get at his thumb and finger.

The old army scout laughed a mirthless laugh as he tried unsuccessfully to peel Calhoun's thumb free.

"That's fine," he said. "I'll just cut off the whole danged hand."

He pressed the blade edge of the Bowie knife against Calhoun's wrist.

***

Daniel and Elijah heard the barking dog and started for the door, convinced it was their father returning home. He'd been gone for days, and though they knew their father sometimes went on long hunts, they were not accustomed to him being away when the snow started like this. Daniel, especially, knew that his father's absence at the first big snow was unusual, and both boys had been on edge, missing their father who threw snowballs with them and eased the burden of their chores by doing half their work.

But Kee Kuttai stopped the boys.

"N'ouvrez pas cette porte," she said. "Do not open that door. Get back until we know who it is."

As she always did when the cur dog started to bark and her husband was not home, Kee Kuttai reached up above the mantle and took down an old scatter gun they kept there.

"Step back now," she said to the boys.

This was not the first time the boys had seen their mother grab the shotgun and step outside to defend the home.

Once, when their father was away on a hunt, a big black bear wandered into the yard. Kee Kuttai had shouted at the bear from the safety of the porch, the door cracked open so that she could flee inside quickly if she had to. The bear had given her a curious glance and then started toward the garden. Kee Kuttai fired a blast from the shotgun into the air, and that had been sufficient to scare away the bear. Another time, she had used the shotgun to put down a wolf threatening the animals in the paddock. Other times the boys had seen their mother sit for hours on the front porch, watching for any threat when the dog was barking or the horses were acting skittish.

So they knew well enough to obey their mother when she told them to step back. They stood by quietly as she pushed aside the heavy bearskin hanging over the doorway as insulation against the cold. She pushed open the door and looked outside. A sick feeling swept through Kee Kuttai, and her heart seemed to leap into her throat, making it hard to breathe. There, off to the side of the house, stepping from the cluster of fir trees, the riderless sorrel horse gave its head a shake and snorted loudly.

"Reste ici," Kee Kuttai said over her shoulder. The boys did not speak much French, except that they recognized phrases their mother often repeated to them. They knew she meant for them to stay put, and they knew when she spoke French at them that she would suffer no argument or disobedience. "Daniel, bar the door behind me."

Kee Kuttai stepped off of the porch, walking cautiously toward the sorrel horse. As she stepped away from the cabin, she heard the heavy board fall in place to bar the door.

The horse had been walking toward the barn, but now it turned toward Kee Kuttai. She noted her husband's Tennessee rifle in its scabbard slid into the saddle straps.

She was not wearing a coat of any kind. She wore only a skirt and a cotton blouse her husband had bought for her down in the town, plenty warm enough inside the cabin, but bitterly insufficient for the winter air outside. The horse, she knew, might have come many miles without a rider. The sorrel with the bone-shaped blaze on his face knew his way home from clear across the valley. The snow slipped inside her moccasins as she stepped off the porch and into the woods, walking toward the firs.

Kee Kuttai gave a shiver as the sorrel horse walked up to her.

She let go of the barrel of the shotgun, and ran her flat her hand over the horse's neck.

"Where's your cavalier?" Kee Kuttai whispered to the horse, a hint of dread in her tone.

She considered leading the horse back to the cabin and tying him to a post while she went inside to get warmer clothes. Then she might ride the horse, doing her best to follow his tracks. The snow was deep enough in most places that she could probably follow the tracks all the way into the valley if she had to.

Had Moses fallen and injured himself? Or had something worse happened?

She almost turned back to the cabin, but then she heard something beyond the fir trees. It sounded like voices, or perhaps just one voice.

From inside the cabin, Kee Kuttai could hear the low growl from the cur dog. She squinted her eyes at the firs, but they stood too thick to see beyond, and so she took up the shotgun again and held it out in front of her, and then she began walking toward the firs.

The snow fell down on her in clumps as she pushed through the thick branches, and then she came out on the other side.

She saw them immediately, about forty yards ahead of her. Two men, both wearing heavy coats made of bearskin. One man on the ground, the other over him, a knife pressed against the injured man on the ground. That's where they were when Kee Kuttai came out of the fir trees and saw them.

She did not immediately recognize her husband. His hat was off him, and what she could see of his face was a bloody mess. But the other man, the man with the knife in his hand, he surely was not Moses Calhoun. He was older, gray-haired with a longer beard, and much heavier than Moses's lean, strong frame.

For just a moment, a heartbeat, Kee Kuttai froze, watching the two men. And then she realized the bloodied, injured man on the ground, was her husband.

The bigger man pressed the blade of his knife against Calhoun's wrist, and Kee Kuttai raised up the shotgun.

"Get off him!" she shouted.

- 25 -

Moses Calhoun felt the pressure lift from his arm.

His face was half pressed into the snow, and Calhoun could still not see a thing. But when he heard Kee Kuttai call out and Bearclaw Jim let go of his arm, Calhoun shifted his arm and wiped his face against his sleeve. The blood was still flowing from his forehead, but he could see, if only for a moment.

"Well now, what's this?" Bearclaw Jim said with a chuckle. "Squaw woman with a gun, eh?"

He stood up, momentarily pressing all of his weight

onto the knee in Calhoun's back, and Moses thought he must have had a broke rib or two for the pain that shot through him. And then Jim was off of him, taking a step or two toward Kee Kuttai.

"What are you going to do with that?" Bearclaw Jim asked. "Going to have a shot at me?"

Calhoun raised up his head, just a touch. They were forty yards out, or thereabout, and Calhoun knew the shotgun was only marginally effective from such a distance. He struggled to catch his breath. He felt like he'd been run over by a buffalo. He had no strength to lift himself. And yet, there in front of him, his wife was in mortal danger. He desperately wanted to call out to her to not fire the gun, not from that range. Likely, she wouldn't do more than enrage Bearclaw Jim, like shooting a grizzly and not killing it. But he could not summon the breath to call out from her.

Instead, Calhoun slid one of his knees under his body. He didn't have strength in his arms to push himself up, and one arm was strapped to his body in a sling. But he had strength in his legs.

Bearclaw Jim took several steps toward Kee Kuttai, but clearly he'd come to the same judgment that Moses Calhoun had reached. Jim knew better than to get too close to the woman with the shotgun, but he also knew that if he could lure her into shooting the gun while he was still at a safe distance, then he would have his way with her.

"Go on and shoot me if that's what you're going to do," Bearclaw Jim taunted. "Cause if you ain't, then I'm going to finish with your man over here."

Jim looked back over his shoulder and saw Calhoun sliding a leg up under him.

"What're you doing there?" Jim said with a chuckle.

He took a step back and again kicked out with his foot, striking Moses Calhoun in the head and knocking the man back down, this time on his side.

"Stop it!" Kee Kuttai shouted again. The flintlock hammer on the scattergun was at full cock. Her finger hovered around the trigger. Seeing the stranger kick her husband almost tempted her to fire the gun, but Moses Calhoun had taught her not to shoot the scattergun from distance. "Even if you're scared," he'd told her, "you wait and shoot when you're sure of killing what you're aiming at."

She was scared now. She was scared at the way her husband's face was covered in blood. She'd never seen him look so weak, so small. He always seemed so big to her, and she felt safe in his arms, safe in his presence, because she knew she could rely on his strength to protect her. But now, kicked by that heavy man with the thick beard and mean face, Moses seemed so weak that she almost could not recognize her own husband.

Bearclaw Jim laughed at her.

"Go on and shoot if you don't like it," he said.

And to taunt her again, he kicked out at Calhoun once more, his boot smashing against Calhoun's arm in the sling.

"Enough!" Kee Kuttai shouted, and now she started toward him. If Bearclaw Jim wouldn't come at her to close the distance, she could do the job herself.

"You best back off, little lady," Bearclaw Jim said, but Kee Kuttai still came at him. She did not run, but her pace was fast enough. She kept the barrel of that scattergun trained on him, too. Her hands were steady like an old gunfighter's, and Bearclaw Jim swallowed hard.

He had no chance if she got within about ten or fifteen yards. She couldn't miss him then. And if she was brave enough to get five yards from him, she'd cut him in half with that damned scattergun. A surge of fear shot through the old army scout as he realized he had brought only a knife to what had become a gunfight.

"You come any closer and I'll put this knife in your man's gut," Bearclaw Jim said, and he raised up the Bowie knife so that she could see it.

But Bearclaw Jim's eyes were on the woman approaching with the scattergun, and he did not see Moses Calhoun's right hand drop to his belt and grasp the head of the hatchet on his belt.

Calhoun slid the hatchet from its place. He gathered up what little strength he had left, and with one, almighty lurch, he swung the hatchet in a sweeping arc, throwing his body with it to extend his range.

The hatchet came down with sickening effect.

The blade struck Bearclaw Jim in the side of his hip, and with the force behind it, ripped muscle and flesh from hip to knee.

Bearclaw Jim howled horrible pain, sounding like an elk on the rut bugling across the valley.

Kee Kuttai broke into a run, handling the scattergun steadily in front of her.

With Calhoun's hatchet locked in joint of his knee, Bearclaw Jim stumbled and then twisted, swiping at Calhoun's wrist with his Bowie knife. Calhoun pulled back, more collapsing than dodging the knife blade. Jim tried to take a step closer to him, but his leg refused to work and he thought he would fall.

And then the squaw was there, six or seven feet away.

Kee Kuttai had the butt of the scattergun in her shoulder, the muzzle perfectly aimed, and she squeezed the trigger.

The shot did not have space between muzzle and target to spread much, and Bearclaw Jim took the full blast in his upper torso, neck, and face. It ripped through his chest and neck and knocked teeth out of his mouth.

He collapsed backward, sucking for air in his final moments.

There was no question for Kee Kuttai whether she'd dealt a mortal blow to her enemy. She'd seen the metal rip apart the man's face and neck.

She tossed the shotgun aside and fell to her knees at her husband's side. His face was bloodied. He cringed with each shallow breath. She could see that he was only just conscious, just able to keep himself aware.

"Moses," she said, and her voice was not more than a hush. "Where are you hurt?"

With the slightest of chuckles, Moses Calhoun moaned, "Everywhere."

- 26 -

Winter brings her heavy snow, beautiful in the way it blankets the valley, but also full of death.

The snow clings to branches and droops the great spruce and fir trees. It piles high on the meadow in the valley, with a soft and almost delicate appearance from above. The grass does not peek through the snow now, and the surface seems smooth and delicate over the rolling hills. When the sun shines, always low on the horizon, all is bright, the sunlight glowing off every surface.

Down in the valley, all is a fight for survival. The wolves fight to catch the weakened elk. The elk fight to get clear of the wolves. The buffalo fight to find the grass. The red fox fight to find the mice. Every animal that calls this place home must wage its own war for survival against the winter freeze.

"Watch your step," Moses Calhoun said, hugging his coat closed around him. "Don't get close to that ledge. It could be slick with ice under the snow."

If the boys were suffering with cabin fever, it was nothing to what Moses Calhoun felt.

For three weeks, Kee Kuttai had hardly allowed him out of bed. Even as his strength began to return and his injuries healed, she still kept him bed-ridden. They slid a cot over near the fire so that Moses would not have to try to maneuver the ladder into the loft, but as he recovered and felt stronger, Kee Kuttai's bothering over him had become a nuisance to him.

But he understood her worry.

After being away for days, he'd returned to his wife bloodied and broken, and her fear of losing her husband had caused her to nurse him with too much vigor. So now, with the sun shining over the frozen mountain and frozen valley, and Moses feeling restored, he decided to walk with his sons to the cliff overlooking the valley. Here, it was his turn to worry overmuch.

"Elijah, son, you stay back from that ledge," Calhoun cautioned again. "Your mama will skin me alive if you drop off of there."

The boys giggled at him, but they heeded his warnings. The cur dog, also eager to get outside and run around a bit, did not come out on the rocky ledge but stayed in the forest, chasing after birds and the scents of a hundred forest animals.

Calhoun surveyed the mountains across the way, covered in white and gleaming in the winter sun. He took a step closer to the ledge, holding his hands out to take hold of his sons. He kicked away the snow piled up high and stomped a foot against the thin layer of ice below to break it up some and make sure he had firm footing. His sons mimicked his movements, though less effective.

"Look down there," Calhoun said, letting go of Daniel's wrist and pointing down into the valley.

Near the stream that ran through the center of the valley was a small herd of buffalo, big and black against the bright snow. The snow behind them looked like the wake of a duck on a lake, broken up and rippled in its own way.

"They're trying to get at the grass," Calhoun said. "Watch the way they shake their heads to get the snow away."

The great beasts broke up the snow, using their powerful neck muscles and their great manes to sweep away the snow and get down to the grass.

The three Calhouns watched the buffalo for a time. There were two dozen or more, all following behind one in a large V-pattern, walking together and breaking up the snow to get at the grass as they slowly made their way through the valley.

Farther up the valley, in the wake of the buffalo, an enormous bull elk sat on the ground, his antlers looking regal over his proud head.

"We get deeper into the winter, he'll get weaker," Calhoun said. "Lack of food, and the energy it takes for him just to stay warm, will make him easy prey for the wolves. But he looks pretty bold now, don't he?"

The boys imagined the wolves coming for the elk, and it gave them both a shiver of fear. Wolves and bear and big cats were the predators the boys most feared, having been so many times cautioned against them by their mother.

"I'm getting cold, Papa," Elijah said.

It amused Moses Calhoun to hear his sons call him "papa." Their mother, raised by her French-Canadian father and his Indian bride, had given the boys plenty of French sayings. "Papa" was among those that sounded foreign to Calhoun's North Carolina ears.

"Yes, sir," Calhoun said. "I reckon we're all getting cold. Let's go back home before your mama starts to worry."

They walked the trail back up to the cabin, stomping with big steps through the thick snow that had managed to find its way through the canopy of trees. All along the way there were branches down, snapped under the weight of the snow, and Calhoun several times stopped to drag one off of the trail.

It felt good to him to move around and pick up heavy things. He'd been too long in bed.

When they got back to the cabin, the boys slid out of their wet boots on the porch and then hurried inside to the warmth of the cabin. Calhoun saw that the door to the smokehouse was cracked open and knew that Kee Kuttai must have gone in there.

"I'll be along presently," he said to his sons.

He went into the smokehouse and found his wife on

her knees, shaving meat into a basket.

Without a word, he put his hands on his wife's back. She twisted around and smiled at him, her eyes alive in the winter sun coming through the door over Calhoun's shoulder.

"Neither of the boys fell over the ledge," Calhoun told her.

"That is good for you," Kee Kuttai said.

Moses slid his hands under her arms and helped Kee Kuttai to her feet, and then he wrapped his arms around her, pulling his wife close to him. He could smell her hair, musky from the smoke. He thought of how Kee Kuttai had rushed out to save him from Bearclaw Jim. She did not shirk the hardships that meant survival for herself, her children, her husband. He thought, too, of the buffalo cows that would push their way through the deep snow to get their calves to pastures where they could feed.

From the lowliest field mouse to the great grizzly, life in these mountains proved harsh, and survival did not come easy.

"It means everything to me to have you here," Moses Calhoun said into his wife's hair. "I couldn't do this without you."

"Pour moi, tu es tout le monde, mon ami," Kee Kuttai said into Calhoun's chest.

They yellow cur dog wandered into the smokehouse, sniffing at the air and getting close to the basket with the meat. The couple broke apart.

"Go on, now," Moses Calhoun said to the dog, scratching it roughly behind the ears. The dog nipped at his hand playfully. It occurred to him that it did not take much for a man in such a hard place to carve out a good life.

the end

ABOUT THE AUTHOR

Robert Peecher is the author of more than a score of Western novels. He is former journalist who spent 20 years working as a reporter and editor for daily and weekly newspapers in Georgia.

Together with his wife Jean, he's raised three fine boys and a mess of dogs. An avid outdoorsman who enjoys hiking trails and paddling rivers, Peecher's novels are inspired by a combination of his outdoor adventures, his fascination with American history, and his love of the one truly American genre of novel: The Western.

For more information and to keep up with his latest releases, we would encourage you to visit his website (mooncalfpress.com) and sign up for his twice-monthly e-newsletter.

OTHER NOVELS BY ROBERT PEECHER

THE LODERO WESTERNS: Two six-shooters and a black stallion. When Lodero makes a graveside vow to track down the mystery of his father's disappearance, it sends Lodero and Juan Carlos Baca on an epic quest through the American Southwest. Don't miss this great 4-book series!

THE TWO RIVERS STATION WESTERNS: Jack Bell refused to take the oath from the Yankees at Bennett Place. Instead, he stole a Union cavalry horse and started west toward a new life in Texas. There he built a town and raised a family, but he'll have to protect his way of life behind a Henry rifle and a Yankee Badge.

ANIMAS FORKS: Animas Forks, Colorado, is the largest city in west of the Mississippi (at 14,000 feet). The town has everything you could want in a Frontier Boomtown: cutthroats, ne'er-do-wells, whores, backshooters, drunks, thieves, and murderers. Come on home to Animas Forks in this fun, character-driven series.

TRULOCK'S POSSE: When the Garver gang guns down the town marshal, Deputy Jase Trulock must form a posse to chase down the Garvers before they reach the outlaw town of Profanity.

FIND THESE AND OTHER NOVELS BY
ROBERT PEECHER AT AMAZON.COM